DARK

INTENTIONS

IRVIN BAXTER

DARK

INTENTIONS

Destiny Image Fiction

An Imprint of
Destiny Image® Publishers, Inc.
P.O. Box 310
Shippensburg, PA 17257-0310

ISBN 0-7684-2071-7

For Worldwide Distribution
Printed in the U.S.A.

1 2 3 4 5 6 7 8 9 10 / 10 09 08 07 06 05 04

This book and all other Destiny Image, Revival Press, MercyPlace, Fresh Bread, Destiny Image Fiction, and Treasure House books are available at Christian bookstores and distributors worldwide.

For a U.S. bookstore nearest you, call
1-800-722-6774.
For more information on foreign distributors, call
717-532-3040.
Or reach us on the Internet:
www.destinyimage.com

Chapter One

It was
a bitterly cold
night. Already,
six inches of snow
had fallen, and the
blustery winds were whip-
ping it into large drifts. The temperature was dropping rapidly toward the zero mark.

Maria Lubenko peered out the window at the fierce
winter storm, thankful she didn't have to go out. "A hot bowl of borscht
and a cup of tea would be perfect for a night like this," she thought to
herself. Maria ladled the soup into one pan, and in another boiled the
water for tea.

After finishing her meal, she settled into her favorite chair by the
fireplace. The heat emanating from the flames penetrated her cold hands
and feet like summer sunshine.

The knock on the door came at 12:01 a.m. Maria knew immediately
what it meant. She had been a midwife for 25 years now. Babies always

chose to be born on nights like this! She opened the door to see Boris Arachev.

His voice was urgent, "Maria, Svetlana is in labor. I'm sorry to make you go out on this horrible night, but I don't know what to do."

"It's alright," she assured him. "Here, come in from the cold." When he stepped inside, the howling wind blew the snow in after him. As Maria put on her boots and heaviest coat, she glanced at the half-finished cup of tea on the table beside her chair. She smiled to herself ruefully, thinking, "Well, it was good while it lasted."

Boris and Maria stepped out into the blasting winter storm. The chilling winds cut like a knife through the midwife's clothing as she and Boris made their way toward the Arachev home. At three or four different places, large snowdrifts blocked their path. Boris plowed through them with his big boots, then returned to help Maria. Several times they lost their footing, falling into the cold snow. Boris and Svetlana's house was only two blocks away, but on this night, it seemed like two miles. Even though Boris knew the neighborhood like the back of his hand, visibility was so bad that, a couple of times, he became disoriented. Fortunately, Maria's sense of direction never failed her.

When they finally reached the front door of the Arachev home, they were nearly frozen. Thankfully, the fire in the fireplace was burning brightly. "Here, give me your coat and hat," Boris said. "Warm yourself for a few minutes by the fire. I'll see to Svetlana."

Maria stood by the fire, absorbing its warmth, until she heard Svetlana cry out. Maria's midwife instincts immediately took over. Entering the bedroom where Svetlana lay, she carefully assessed the situation. Asking all the normal questions, Maria estimated the baby would be born within two or three hours.

It wasn't an easy birth, and took much longer than Maria had expected. Six grueling hours later, the baby was ready to be born. By then, Svetlana was soaked with perspiration and weary to the bone.

When Maria saw the face of the 8 pound, 9 ounce boy, she was startled. Of all places, a birthmark was clearly visible on his forehead! His dark, intelligent eyes appeared to immediately take in everything in the room. During all of her years as a midwife, she had never seen anything quite like it!

Maria gently placed the newborn on Svetlana's stomach. The new mother smiled wearily, but with eyes of joy. "Oh, a baby boy!" she exclaimed. Then she saw the birthmark. "Oh my," she cried in concern. "Is he all right? I've never seen anyone with a birthmark there. It's not an evil omen, is it?"

"No, no," Maria assured her. "He's a perfectly normal child. Birthmarks can be anywhere."

The smile returned to Svetlana's face. "Look at the devilment in those eyes! No wonder I had such a difficult pregnancy and birth!"

Maria took the child and began to wash him at the large kitchen sink. When she washed his hair, her attention was riveted to the large birthmark on his forehead. A shudder of trepidation ran through her. "Stop it," she scolded herself. "All that superstitious nonsense means nothing. Stalin has told us there is no God, and there certainly is no devil." Still, she couldn't shake the nagging feeling of foreboding. She found herself wanting to complete her duties and get back to the safety of her own home.

Maria wrapped the baby in a clean blanket and handed him to his father. The newborn didn't like his daddy's touch and began screaming angrily. "What a temper!" Boris said. As soon as the midwife took the baby back, he calmed down.

Maria and Boris returned to Svetlana's side. When she saw her baby, she smiled brightly. Taking him into her arms, she looked into his face and said, "Hello, Michael."

"So you've already decided on a name," Maria commented. "Michael is a nice name." To herself, Maria thought, "That's the only thing normal about this child."

With a smile, Maria said, "Well, my work is done. I'm going to get back to my house and get a little sleep."

Boris protested, "It's too cold outside. We have an extra bed. Why don't you rest here for a while?"

Maria replied quickly—she hoped not too quickly, "No. The wind has died down, and since it is light, I'll be able to see. I must get back."

As she stuck her head back into Svetlana's room to check on her one last time, baby Michael's eyes followed her every move. "What is it about those eyes?" Maria thought uneasily. "They are so piercing and too intelligent for a newborn baby." As Maria stepped out into the crisp morning air, she couldn't shake the fear this child evoked within her. "It's that birthmark on his forehead," she rationalized. Still, she found herself walking as fast as she could.

Chapter Two

After the birth of their son, Michael, life settled back to normal for Boris and Svetlana Arachev. Living under the regime of Joseph Stalin was uncertain at best. However, their little farm in southern Russia, 50 miles south of the city of Volgograd, was quite far removed from the political intrigue of Moscow.

Young Michael was a joy to Boris and Svetlana, even though at times he could be a handful. He was a brilliant child of boundless energy, and it quickly became obvious to all around him that he was a born leader.

Michael was eight years old when World War II broke out. That night after dinner, his dad and Grandpa Arachev sat around the dining room table for several hours pouring over the articles about Hitler's invasion of Poland, and discussing the potential effects upon the Soviet Union. Though concerned about this development, there was a feeling these events would never reach all the way down to Volgograd.

Even at his young age, Michael sensed something very important was transpiring; however, he didn't fully comprehend the ramifications of war at the time.

In spite of the war, life didn't change much for the Arachevs until two years later when Hitler launched his invasion of the Soviet Union. By this time Michael was older, and able to somewhat understand the gravity of the new situation. He listened intently as his dad, mom, grandpa, and grandma talked that evening.

"That double-crossing Hitler!" Grandpa exclaimed. "Signing a non-aggression pact with our leader Stalin, and then launching a surprise attack against us. What treachery!"

"Is there a chance Hitler's troops could penetrate into the heartland and actually invade Volgograd?" Boris asked his father apprehensively.

"Oh, I don't think so," came the confident reply from Grandpa Arachev. "Comrade Stalin would never allow that to happen."

"But Germany's blitzkrieg attack has demolished every enemy in Hitler's way so far," Boris reminded his father. "I've never seen anything like it."

"Everything will be fine," Grandpa Arachev assured, attempting to allay the fears that he sensed were growing in each family member. "Germany has yet to face the mighty Russian bear. We may not be the fastest army in the world, but we keep moving forward, day after day."

The Germans advanced into Russian territory much more swiftly than the Russians had thought possible. When news reached Volgograd that the German forces were only one hundred miles away, the tension and concern in the Arachev home was written on each of the adults' faces. As much as Boris and Svetlana tried, they were not able to shield Michael from an awareness of the impending danger.

At night, after young Michael was sent off to bed, Grandpa and Grandma Arachev would sit around the kitchen table with Boris and Svetlana discussing the ever-increasing seriousness of the military situation.

What they didn't know was that Michael would slip out of bed and listen intently to these late-night conversations through the keyhole of the door.

As Michael listened one particular night, the discussion turned extraordinarily urgent. He heard his father say to Grandpa Arachev, "The Germans could be here within three or four days. Dad, what do you think they will do to us?"

There was a long pause before Grandpa Arachev answered. "I've been reading the papers and listening carefully to the news. In most places where the Germans have invaded, they have not actually been slaughtering our people. They confiscate food and any guns that they find. But as long as individuals have not resisted, they have usually been left alone."

"So what should we be doing in preparation for the invasion?" Svetlana asked anxiously.

Grandpa Arachev explained, "It's important that we protect our food supply. We will have to find a way to hide most of what we have and still leave enough in our houses so the Germans won't know that we have hidden our stockpile."

"What about our savings?" Boris inquired.

"The same thing applies there," Grandpa Arachev replied confidently. "We have to protect most of what we have while, at the same time, not arouse suspicion that there may be more."

Then came the question that everyone was dreading to ask. "Is there any danger that you and Boris might be taken away?" Svetlana asked, trying, but failing to hide the fear in her voice.

There was a very long pause before the reply came. Michael strained to catch every word. Finally, it was Boris who spoke, "We want to believe that won't happen, but we have to be realistic. It appears the Germans have been taking some of the men that are considered community leaders. Apparently, they want to prevent the organization of resistance to their occupation."

Grandma Arachev turned to her husband, attempting to make her point courageously, "So, since you are on the governing council for this province, you could well be targeted." It was more of a statement than a question.

Grandpa Arachev replied matter-of-factly, "I'm sure this is a possibility, however, we'll have to deal with that if and when the time comes."

From his listening post in the laundry room, Michael tried to assimilate what he was hearing. It suddenly dawned on him how serious their situation really was.

Michael could sense the strength of character in his mother, as she spoke bravely. "We can't wait to see what might happen. We have to plan for all eventualities. How will we deal with it if they do take Grandpa Arachev away? What if they take Boris as well? What will we need to do to hold things together until this horrible nightmare is over?"

The discussion continued late into the night. When Michael finally slipped into bed, sleep wouldn't come. The thought of his grandpa, and maybe his father, being hauled away by the Germans tortured his young mind. He was still tossing and turning when the light of dawn began to filter through his bedroom window.

Michael would never forget the day the German armies swept through the province where their little farm was located. Most of the people stayed huddled in their houses hoping to be left alone. Every few minutes they would sneak a peak through the shutters to see what was happening outside. German jeeps, tanks and supply trucks could be seen moving steadily up and down the streets, supporting the front lines.

On the third day of the occupation, Michael heard his dad say to his mother, "I have to go see about my parents. I want to be sure they are all right."

"But Boris," Michael heard his Mother ask anxiously, "what if the Germans take you away?"

"I don't think they will," Boris replied reassuringly. "They have a war to fight. It doesn't appear that they are looking for prisoners."

Michael waited all day long for his father to return with news about his grandpa. Michael loved his grandpa so much! What would he do if the Germans had taken him away?

Michael's apprehension grew stronger and stronger as the day wore on. His father still had not returned by bedtime. Finally, his mother told him it was time to go to bed.

"No. I'm staying up till Dad gets home," Michael protested.

"You can't do that," Svetlana stated flatly. "Your father might have to spend the night with Grandma and Grandpa. We don't know what the situation might be with the Germans. You'll need your rest for tomorrow. Good night."

Michael went to bed, but he didn't go to sleep. He couldn't. Finally, sometime after midnight, he dozed off.

About one o'clock in the morning, he heard the front door of their house open. Springing out of bed, he heard his father's voice. "The Germans have taken Dad into custody. I thought it would be best to bring Mother here until this whole thing blows over."

Michael came bursting out of his room. "Where is Grandpa Arachev? Where have they taken him?" he screamed. The rage Michael felt toward the Germans was so intense he could not control it. "Tell me," he demanded. "I'm going to go get him right now!"

"Calm down, Michael," his Mother said, attempting to quiet him.

"Don't treat me like a baby!" Michael cried. "That's my grandpa! Why do people have to fight wars anyway?"

Boris Arachev placed a hand on his son's shoulder. "I don't blame you for the way you feel. He's my father, and I am very angry. However, there's nothing we can do about it right now. I'm sure your grandpa will be home before very long. We will have to be patient. In the meantime, you and I have to take care of Grandma Arachev and your mother. Go back to bed."

When Michael finally returned to his room, all he could think about was his grandpa in a German prison camp. His mind raced as he attempted to come to grips with his grandpa's arrest. Grandpa hadn't done anything! It wasn't fair!"

Michael slept very little that night. He paced back and forth in his room, his mind racing. He looked out the window for a while, hoping that an answer might come to him as he stared into the night. He even tried praying to God. The teachers at school had told him there was no God, however, he had wondered, "If there is no God, why do they spend so much time trying to convince everyone that God doesn't exist?"

Around three o'clock in the morning, Michael fell into a restless sleep. He dreamed of his grandpa in the German prison camp. He saw German troops marching, shouting, "Sieg Heil!"

At 4 a.m., Michael awoke from his troubled dreams. Sitting straight up in bed, it was as though all the confusion had evaporated from his young mind. He could see what needed to be done as clear as crystal. War was insane! It should be outlawed...declared illegal. Why did Germans have to fight Russians or French or British? They didn't! Why couldn't the world simply unite—become one? If there were one worldwide government, the root cause for conflict would be removed. Furthermore, if there were a global government, then there would only be one army. A single, unified, worldwide military wouldn't fight with itself. Michael saw it so clearly! Sitting there in his bed, he said aloud, "It's stupid, small-minded nationalism that causes all the world's conflicts."

It suddenly seemed so simple. Michael knew in that instant he would never rest until the world was revolutionized, placing mankind under the canopy of an all-encompassing world government. War would then be banished forever.

Michael's vision crystallized into resolve that night. He knew he was right, and, one day, the world would know it too! He drifted off to sleep, knowing that the course of his life was set. He had stared destiny in the face, and he liked what he saw.

Four months passed before any news arrived from Grandpa Arachev. The letter that came was somewhat reassuring. "I am doing fine. Do not worry about me. I don't know yet when I will be able to come home, but it probably won't be for a while." It was the P.S. that riveted Michael's attention. "Tell Michael I love him. It will be up to him and his generation to find a new way to run the world so that we won't have these senseless wars anymore." Michael had not disclosed to anyone the feelings of destiny he had recently experienced. Now he wondered if his grandpa somehow knew about his "special calling."

Chapter Three

Michael's teenage years passed swiftly. So many Russian men had been called-up by the military that teenage boys had to bear the burden of raising crops. Besides this, there was school.

Michael loved school. He wanted to know and understand everything. His keen mind devoured history. Little by little, he formed his personal opinions as to why the world was the way it was and what should be done to fix it. Most of his friends were interested in typical youthful pursuits, but Michael couldn't get enough of politics and world affairs. His sense of destiny drove him with the urgency of a raging inner hunger!

When it came time to study the *Communist Manifesto* and *Das Kapital*, most of his classmates groaned, but Michael absorbed these founding teachings of socialism like a sponge. He believed a perfect world could be created by applying the principles taught by Karl Marx. He dreamed of the day when there would be a one-world socialistic government. And he knew that he was the one who would finally bring that dream to reality.

Because of his high marks and his excellence in political subjects, Michael was accepted into Moscow University to study law. He knew if he were going to rule the world he would need to understand the intricacies of law, since laws control human behavior. In college his global plan began to take shape.

Michael was so excited the day he entered his first semester political science class. His professor, Alexander Sobchak, proved to be brilliant educator! Professor Sobchak opened the first class with a matter of fact statement. "Ladies and gentlemen, it is inevitable that communism will ultimately rule the world. One of you in this class may end up ruling over a World Union of Socialist Republics. If that comes to pass, you must first understand one thing. There are three root causes of war in our world: political conflicts, economic conflicts and religious conflicts. If world peace is ever to be attained, there will have to be a one-world government, a one-world economy and a global religious system."

Sobchak continued, "Now this may not be as difficult as it seems at first glance. Much of the preparatory work has already been done for this new global system. When the United Nations was established in 1945, it was specifically designed to be a socialist world government. Alger Hiss, who was appointed by Roosevelt, Stalin and Churchill to write the UN's charter, built the structure for world government and a global economy into the document. However, he was unable to deal with the religious component since the world's thinking was not yet sufficiently conditioned to adopt a global spirituality."

Excitement surged through Michael as he absorbed what Professor Sobchak was explaining. "Why, the foundation for my global government has already been laid!" he exclaimed to himself. All doubt regarding his role in the fulfillment of destiny left him. However, he noted that religious union was a critical issue, and would have to be dealt with.

Professor Sobchak's lecture continued as Michael sat enthralled. "As all of you know, the Politburo is where power resides in the Soviet Union. The UN Security Council is designed to be a global politburo. We have one critical obstacle to overcome. The United States was unwilling to place absolute power in the hands of the Security Council. In order to protect their sovereignty, they insisted on veto power over the Council's decisions. Before world government can be fully implemented, that veto power must be abolished."

Michael raised his hand. "Yes, Michael?" Professor Sobchak asked.

"Professor Sobchak, why do you assume our side would win if the veto power were abolished? The capitalists are still in the majority, and the message of capitalism is still very powerful in our world. Do you believe the time will come that the socialist ideal could be the victor in a global democratic election?"

Sobchak was impressed with the depth of perception indicated by the question. It was unusual in a first-year student. "Excellent question, Michael, and a very important one. The time will come much sooner than you think, when the majority of the world will favor the economic system of socialism."

Michael interrupted, "How can that possibly be true seeing that most of the world presently lives under capitalism?"

"There's something you don't know, Michael. From the beginning of the Communist Revolution, we have concentrated on infiltrating the educational systems of the world. We have installed our fellow travelers on school boards, in college presidencies, and we plan to maneuver ourselves into positions that will allow us to revise most of the textbooks. We also have concentrated on gaining control of the media. The entire purpose is to slowly change the minds of the people of the world.

"While the West is concentrating on winning the arms race, we have been winning the battle for the mind. Never forget it! The pen is mightier than the sword."

"Wow!" Michael thought to himself. "This is going to happen!"

In Professor Sobchak, Michael found a true mentor. He often stayed long after class, discussing the worldwide advances of communism and the overall global situation. These private conversations were real eye-openers for Michael and reinforced his conviction that the Marxist dream of one-world government could be achieved in his lifetime.

One particular evening Michael said to Professor Sobchak, "From all I read and hear, anti-communist sentiments are still very strong in the western world."

The professor smiled. "Michael, you must understand something. The West is concerned about labels and slogans. We care nothing about those things. All we care about is the realization of our Marxist dreams. We will gradually convert the Western world into a socialistic system while they continue to think that it is capitalism. We don't care what they call it as long as we accomplish our purpose."

"But how could that possibly be done?" Michael asked, intrigued.

"In fact, it is already being done," Sobchak replied. "Through our American and European agents, we have been successful in introducing socialist forms of government into the governments of the West."

Michael began to understand. "Are you speaking of social security, welfare, the graduated income tax, ever-increasing governmental regulation and things of that nature?" he inquired.

"Absolutely," Professor Sobchak replied with satisfaction as he watched understanding dawn on his favorite pupil's face. "We will back the West into socialism until they choose our system for themselves in democratic elections."

Michael's inquiries continued, "So at what level of taxation does a country become a de facto socialist state?"

"Insiders here believe it occurs when a country's rate of taxation of its citizens' incomes reaches fifty percent," Sobchak disclosed.

Michael's eyes narrowed as he spoke quietly, "Professor Sobchak, you know an awful lot about the inside workings of the governmental power structure. You even referred to 'insiders' awhile ago. Who are they?"

Sobchak slowly smiled. "You don't fool this young man much," he thought to himself. Then he said, "Michael, I believe you are truly committed to the cause of socialism and the Marxist dream, or I would not tell you these things.

"No man on earth could run the government of a country by himself. It's too complex. Consequently, there must be groups that prepare young people like yourself for leadership. These groups also serve as think tanks to privately advise our national leaders, especially concerning foreign affairs. These think tanks do not only exist in our country, but in every major country in the world. These centers of power are aware of one another and interact with one another—unofficially, of course."

Then came the question Michael was dying to ask, "Are you one of these insiders? Are you a member of one of these think tanks?"

"Michael, I cannot answer that question unless I swear you to absolute secrecy," Professor Sobchak replied seriously.

Michael's reply was immediate, "Professor, you know you can trust me."

"I believe you, Michael. But you must understand that, when you get near the center of power in our world, confidences must be taken very seriously," Sobchak warned. "Some things are so critical that, if anyone entrusted with them discloses them, he might even have to be eliminated. Do you understand?"

"Yes sir. Of course I do," Michael's answer came without hesitation.

Professor Sobchak continued, "When a careless statement to the press or an inappropriate disclosure in an interview could change the course of world history and set back the cause of world government for a decade, the highest level of accountability is essential. Do you understand?"

"Yes, sir."

"All right, I'll tell you," the professor continued. "I am a member of what is called the Council on Foreign Affairs. We bring young potential leaders up through our ranks, preparing them to assume power. We make sure they embrace the right values and will move the world steadily toward our planned New World Order. Since its inception, every Minister of Foreign Affairs of the Soviet Union has come from the Council on Foreign Affairs."

"Is the Council on Foreign Affairs a governmental agency, or is it a private club?"

"It is a private club, but very well-connected," Sobchak explained.

"So this is, in reality, sort of an invisible government," Michael commented as comprehension slowly dawned on him. "And you say there are think tanks like this in most major countries?"

"Yes, there are."

"What is it called in the United States," Michael wanted to know.

"Actually, it's almost the same as it is here in the Soviet Union. In the U.S. it is called the Council on Foreign Relations," Sobchak explained.

As Michael left Professor Sobchak's house that evening, his head was spinning with the day's disclosures. He was sobered by the intricacies of the power structures that ruled his nation, and obviously the world. It also was apparent to him that at least one insider felt he was a suitable candidate to become a future world leader.

Chapter Four

In his senior year of college, Michael's life took a sudden and unexpected turn. Visiting the library the day before the first semester actually began, he was reading one of the latest commentaries on *Das Kapital*. Momentarily glancing up from his book, he saw the most beautiful girl he had ever seen in his life sitting at the next table. In that instant she happened to look in his direction. She smiled at him. Her mouth was full, generous and appealing, and her eyes were the coolest emerald green color. Michael caught himself staring. It had been so long since he had "noticed" a girl that he didn't know exactly how to react. He quickly lowered his eyes back to his book and acted as though it hadn't happened.

Later that afternoon, as he walked back to his apartment, the vision of those green eyes and that appealing smile repeatedly invaded his thoughts. "I don't have time for romance," he said to himself. "My studies must take absolute priority in my life right now. Besides, I'll probably never see her again." Try as he might, Michael could not push her out of his mind. She danced in and out of his dreams all night long.

Michael prepared for class the next morning with great enthusiasm. His first class was Advanced Studies of Vladimir Lenin with Professor Lubenko. He had heard that Professor Lubenko was one of the foremost experts in the world on the life and teachings of Lenin. Since Lenin was his most revered revolutionary leader, Michael entered the class with eager anticipation.

Walking into the classroom, Michael's eyes quickly searched for Professor Lubenko. However, the professor had obviously not yet arrived. Looking for a seat near the front of the class where he always liked to sit, his gaze suddenly settled on the girl he had seen in the library the night before. It shocked Michael when his heart leaped and his brain temporarily refused to function. These reactions were so foreign to him! All of his life he had felt nothing but supreme self-confidence. He was so befuddled he bumped into one of the front row desks, knocking it sideways. He paused a moment, regaining control. When he looked up, the girl with the generous smile spoke to him, "Hi. Didn't I see you in the library last night?"

By now Michael had regained his composure. "Yes, I think you did. What a coincidence that we would be in the same first class!" he replied.

"I think that chair is free. You can sit there if you want to." It was both an invitation and a challenge.

Michael sat down. "Great," he thought to himself. "I dream of this girl all night long. I can't get her out of my mind. Then I come to the most important class of my college career, and I find myself sitting right beside her. This can't be good." While he was thinking these thoughts to himself, an excitement was building within him that he could not deny.

Professor Lubenko entered the room. In spite of his long anticipation of meeting the professor, Michael had to force himself to keep his eyes on him. He found himself continually casting sidelong glances toward the beautiful girl on his left.

"It must be understood," Lubenko began, "that personalities sometime distort the true nature of the Marxist revolution. Stalin did much to advance the cause of the socialist movement, but he also resorted to many abuses that cannot be justified."

Then came the shocking revelation. "All of us have known that many good patriots were victimized by the abuses of Stalin's regime, but the extent of these abuses of power have only recently been revealed. Ladies and gentlemen, twenty million Soviet citizens were exterminated during Stalin's political purges. Some of these actions may have been justifiable, but twenty million murders in the name of the revolution are simply beyond the pale! We can no longer whitewash these atrocities and pretend they didn't happen. If we care about our beloved revolution, we must take measures to ensure that these barbarous actions will never be allowed again in the name of government!"

Rada Aleksandrov, the girl Michael had met at the library, broke in with a question. "Professor, what flaw in our system allowed these levels of abuse to occur? There must be something fundamental that needs to be corrected."

"This is the point that must be considered," Lubenko agreed. "The fact is that there is nothing wrong with our socialist system—as it was originally conceived. It was Stalin's distortion of the system that has produced this scandal. Lenin never intended for abuses of power like this to be possible. You will notice in his writings he always spoke of 'Democratic Socialism.'

"If we are to see the successful conclusion of our world revolution, we will have to forsake the concept of a 'dictatorship of the proletariat' in favor of democratic socialism."

Michael interrupted, "But how could that ever work? The uneducated masses are so easily manipulated."

Professor Lubenko nodded, "You are right, of course. But that is exactly why it will work. Those most skilled at guiding the opinion of the masses will end up ruling the world. Here in the Soviet Union we are masters at giving guidance to the press in order to lead society in the way it should go."

"But that is possible because we do not have the Western tradition of freedom of the press," Michael argued. "How would we ever implement this on a global scale?"

"The key is to guide the press without appearing to," Lubenko explained. "This is done by making sure the major media outlets are owned by people who share our political ideals. They, in turn, will hire people who mirror their values."

Rada raised her hand, "The American people are almost evenly divided between liberal and conservative. Yet I read recently that eighty-five percent of the media vote liberal. Is this liberal bias in the media what you are speaking of, and is the hand of the revolution secretly behind this?"

Lubenko lowered his voice conspiratorially, "That is exactly what I am saying. But let me caution you...it would not serve the cause of the revolution if you discussed these things openly, especially in venues that might appear in print in the West."

Michael understood! There were a million pieces to the puzzle of world government that would ultimately come together. And none of it was happening by accident. It was all part of a well-thought-out intricate plan. The average person would never even know it was happening. But the insiders knew. Of that, Michael was sure...and he realized he was becoming one of the insiders.

As the semester progressed, for the first time Michael was not at the top of his class. However, it was not because he wasn't performing up to his usual stellar standards. He was. One student outscored him – the girl who haunted his dreams – Rada Aleksandrov. He quickly found she was as brilliant as she was beautiful.

Professor Lubenko's lectures lived up to all that Michael had heard about them, and he was almost certain that Lubenko was one of the insiders.

For some time, Michael had been looking for an opportunity to invite Rada out for a date. One Monday morning, an announcement on the college bulletin board caught his attention–Politburo member Andrei Gorky to lecture on 'Socialism and Spirituality.' "This is the perfect chance," he thought.

After Lubenko's class that day, Michael caught up with Rada in the hall. "What are you doing Thursday evening?" he inquired. "Would you considering going somewhere with me?"

Rada paused thoughtfully. She had promised to be at her friend Yalena's house for dinner that evening, but Yalena would understand if she cancelled. Rada had wondered how long it would take Michael to finally ask her out. The attraction between them had become more and more powerful as the semester progressed. She moved to one side of the hall where they could stop and talk. Flashing that gorgeous smile at Michael, she said, "Sure. I'd love to. What do you have in mind?"

"Well, if you'd like to, I do have something in mind. I noticed on the bulletin board that Politburo member Andrei Gorky will be speaking at 7 p.m. on 'Socialism and Spirituality.' It's a subject I've been interested in for a long time."

"I'd love to do that," Rada responded.

"One more thing," Michael continued. "Is there any time at all before then that we could get together? I have some thoughts on the role of spirituality in the Marxist revolution that I would like to discuss with you before we actually hear the lecture."

"How about Wednesday afternoon at 3," Rada suggested. "I think we're both done with classes by then, aren't we?"

"I'll meet you in the park down by the Lenin Monument," Michael said. "That would be the perfect place to talk."

"See you then, Michael," Rada said warmly, as she walked away.

As Michael headed toward his next class, he felt as though he had entered another world. The overwhelming attraction he felt for Rada defied explanation. He tried to rationalize it. He tried to explain it away. None of that worked. But Michael knew it was definitely real, for it pulled at something deep within him day and night.

Three o'clock Wednesday was all he could think about as he slipped into the chair for his class on international finance. Between Monday and Wednesday, the hours seemed to drag even though Michael was very busy.

He arrived at the monument 10 minutes early. Michael liked to be early for everything he did. He found himself wondering where she was, and it wasn't even three o'clock yet. "Calm down," he told himself. "Are you falling in love?"

When Rada didn't show up at three, Michael's agitation was hard to control. "Where is she?" he wondered. "Maybe she started thinking about it and changed her mind." At 3:03, Michael thought perhaps she had misunderstood the meeting place. But how could she? There was only one Lenin Monument in the park. At 3:05, he almost decided that perhaps he was wrong about her. "I was sure she was as attracted to me as I was to her. But, why would she be late? Why, I was ten minutes early!" He thought of leaving, but he couldn't. "Maybe something beyond her control had happened."

At exactly 3:07, Rada came walking up the sidewalk toward the monument. Michael's nature was to take her to task for being late. But when he saw her, he couldn't. "Hi, Michael," Rada greeted him as though nothing was wrong. "Isn't it a beautiful day?" she asked looking right into his eyes.

"Ten minutes late...ten minutes early...what did it matter?" Michael thought to himself. She was here. That's all that mattered anyway.

"You are so beautiful," he said before he even realized he was going to say it.

Rada's green eyes sparkled, "Why thank you, Michael. What a nice thing for you to say!"

For the next hour Michael learned all that he could about Rada. "Where are you from? Do you have brothers and sisters? Where did you attend secondary school? How did you end up at Moscow University? What are your goals and dreams?"

Nearly an hour had passed when Rada smiled and said mischievously, "I thought you invited me here to discuss tomorrow night's lecture on 'Socialism and Spirituality'."

Grinning broadly, Michael explained, "Well, I meant to, but you got me off track. I do want to discuss that with you. Let me explain why.

"In the first semester of my freshman year, I had a professor named Sobchak. He first taught that there are three forces on earth that must be unified in order to bring about our goal of one-world government. He explained that there must be a global political system, a global economy and a global spirituality or belief system.

"He went on to describe how the United Nations was structured to fulfill the drive into one-world government and one-world economy. But he said it was not possible to lay the groundwork for the global spirituality at the time the UN was born. That's the reason this lecture being given tomorrow night attracted me so much."

"How interesting," Rada responded. "I knew the UN was designed to be a world government, but I didn't realize the structure for a world economy was included in that."

"Oh definitely," Michael affirmed. "At the Bretton Woods Conference in 1944, the World Bank was born and the International Monetary Fund (IMF) was established. The IMF is destined to become the Federal Reserve Bank of the world. The founding fathers of the UN knew at that time that you couldn't have a world government without a world economic system."

Michael continued, "What I am attempting to envision is how this world, with all of its extremely diverse religious beliefs, could ever be led into a global spirituality."

"Now I understand why tomorrow night's lecture is going to be so very important," Rada said enthusiastically.

Around five o'clock she said, "Michael, I've got to be going. I have work that has to be done."

"You have to stay seven more minutes," Michael informed her. "You were seven minutes late, you know."

"Was I?" Rada queried, her eyes dancing mischievously.

After they parted, Michael couldn't get her out of his mind. He felt like a chess player that had been outplayed. Rada had not admitted it, but he suspected that she had been late on purpose. She acted as though she didn't even realize it. "Are all females this maddening?" he wondered to himself, smiling. Already he couldn't wait for tomorrow night to come.

Chapter Five

Michael and Rada had been schooled in the Marxist belief that there was no God, and that religion was merely the 'opium of the people.' Their parents had conveyed certain religious beliefs to them, which had been held before the Communist Revolution in the Soviet Union. However, Rada and Michael had long since divorced themselves from any religious sensibilities whatsoever.

For three years, Michael had been attempting to understand how the religious issue could be dealt with when the inevitable New World Order was established. If religious conflict was the number one cause of war on earth, then it had to be resolved. But how? He entered the lecture hall on Thursday hoping to get some answers from Politburo member Gorky's lecture on 'Socialism and Spirituality.'

Michael and Rada settled into their places, pen and paper in hand. The KGB was much in evidence everywhere in the room. As Andrei Gorky strode to the podium, a hush settled over the hall.

Immediately, Gorky launched into his lecture. "Fellow comrades, one very important thing must be clearly understood. One overriding issue will determine the success or failure of our sacred revolution. The battle will be won or lost in the realm of the spiritual.

"Contrary to what many of you have believed, our goal is not to defeat capitalism." Gorky paused a long time to allow the impact of what he had said to sink in. Rada and Michael looked at each other inquisitively. Gorky continued, "No. Our goal is not to defeat capitalism. Our goal is to abolish Judeo-Christian values. Once the Judeo-Christian value system is destroyed, capitalism will collapse of its own accord.

"Let me explain. People inherently either place their faith in God to solve their problems or they place their faith in government. Once faith in God is undermined, people automatically look to government for answers. They even begin to demand that government take responsibility for their well-being.

"Why is this true, and why is it so important?" Gorky asked rhetorically. "Socialism is the only political and economic doctrine that can ever lead mankind to perfection. Socialism provides for total control by the government, leaving nothing to chance. Ultimately, we will have a law to control everything and every situation.

"On the other hand, capitalism is a system of free enterprise. It depends on the people governing themselves. The fewer laws you have, the more dynamically it works. Capitalism and democracy, in theory, is self-government...government 'of the people, by the people and for the people.' The only way this ridiculous form of government has any chance of working at all is when religion induces the populace to control natural selfish inclinations and to 'do unto others as they would have others do to them.'

"Ladies and gentlemen, we can never risk the future of our world on imaginary edicts of faith! We must deal with reality! Once mankind realizes that there is no God, then we will take the proper responsibility for our own future. Then our world will understand that humanism, or communism as some call it, holds the key to the future of our planet. As long as people look to God for their answers, they will never be willing to put the necessary trust in government."

Michael concentrated furiously on what Andrei Gorky was saying. "So that's the reason I resent it so much when believers say 'I'll pray about it.' Human beings must assume responsibility for their own destiny, not wait for some God who doesn't exist to solve their problems!" he mused to himself.

After the speech, Rada and Michael left the lecture hall. Rada could tell that something was bothering Michael. When they came to Trotsky Park, she took him by the hand, leading him to a nearby bench.

Pulling him down beside her, she probed, "Well, what did you think of Comrade Gorky's speech?"

Michael's reply came slowly, pensively. "I believe what we have been taught...that religion is the opium of the people. Yet, I also believe there is a spiritual dimension to some of the problems we are facing in our world. I guess the thing that bothers me most is that I don't see us being able to stamp out religion in this generation. Religious beliefs, in most parts of the world, are held more dearly than political beliefs.

"We believe we will see the establishment of the Marxist New World Order in our lifetime. Yet, how do you go about cleansing a world from religious superstition when it is absolutely awash with it? Is such a thing even possible?"

Suddenly, the lights came on in Rada's brain. "You know, Michael, sometimes things that appear to be our greatest obstacles can actually become our greatest assets. Perhaps there is actually a way to use religious loyalties to bring the world together rather than attempting to eradicate religion completely. We may be beating our heads against a wall that cannot be moved."

The moment she said it, Michael knew that Rada was right. While he didn't see how it could be accomplished, he instinctively knew that this was the path the world must take. He now understood what must be done even though he did not yet see exactly how to do it.

Chapter Six

Rada and Michael were married shortly after their graduation from college. In Rada, Michael had not only found a beautiful companion, but a political soul mate as well. She became his closest friend and his most trusted political counselor.

Michael's rise to power in the Soviet Union was nothing short of meteoric. His absolute sense of destiny served to set him apart from all other politicians. He was never caught unprepared, because he knew exactly where he was going long before he ever got there. As a result, plans were in place far in advance. Each time he assumed a new position, the plan of action kicked in like a whirlwind. This inspired tremendous awe in his followers and caught his enemies off guard. He moved so swiftly that the battles were over before opponents even understood where the lines of attack were.

Michael became the youngest man ever chosen to become a member of the Soviet Union's Politburo. He quickly ingratiated himself to the older Politburo members. His willingness to tackle jobs that no one else wanted, his razor-sharp mind and his winning smile won over his enemies. It soon became apparent to everyone that here was an extraordinarily gifted leader who would someday become president of the Soviet Union.

The day came sooner than Michael expected. Several of the elderly presidents blocking his path died in rapid succession. Arachev was chosen as leader of the USSR.

To most politicians, becoming the leader of a nation was the ultimate prize. However, to Michael it was only a stepping-stone. He tackled the archaic structures of the Soviet Union with his usual speed and energy. Obstacles that past leaders of the Soviet Union had struggled with for decades were dispatched within a few short months. Michael would simply tolerate no interference. He knew exactly where he was going and how he intended to get there. The Arachev Era could not be described as anything short of revolutionary.

Three years into his presidency, Arachev's power was absolute. Every political enemy had been vanquished, allowing him to move forward with his global plan unchallenged. He proceeded to delegate power on the national level so that he could enact his plan to capture power at the world level. He understood that he could not move on to the next level of power until he had successfully trained and installed national leaders who could be counted on to cooperate fully with his global agenda.

Meticulously, Michael and Rada hammered out the next phase of Arachev's ascent to global power. He would lay out his plan for her, and she would analyze its strengths and weaknesses. Together they massaged the blueprint they had created until they were certain that every flaw had been carefully worked out.

Then came the secret meetings. Arachev confided his plan individually to the key members of the Politburo, overcoming their objections one by one. He knew in advance what the objections would be and what the answers were. He and Rada had already gone over each of them numerous times.

Successful delegation required an in-depth understanding of human nature. People needed to be placed in positions that would suit their unique combination of strengths and weaknesses perfectly. Strengths had to be suited to carrying out the responsibilities of the task. Weaknesses were to be exploited to keep the person under control.

This was where Michael excelled. Not only had he been born with an innate ability to judge the character of a person, but he had also finely honed this skill throughout his political career.

Once all the groundwork had been laid, the Politburo meeting was convened in which the entire plan would be presented and adopted. As the members entered one by one, Arachev greeted them warmly, mentally going over the role that each would be expected to play. Most of them were handpicked, people he had carefully brought up through the ranks. He knew them like the back of his hand. Not only did he know what they could do, he also knew what they wouldn't or couldn't do.

Many of them were at the top of their political careers and knew it. They enjoyed their jobs and were addicted to the perks that went with them. They were the bean counters, the education ministers—the bureaucrats that made the government machinery function. Then there were the key influencers and the potential future leaders.

When Alexei Tregub entered, Arachev bowed his head respectfully. Tregub held the portfolio of Minister of Agriculture. His fellow Politburo members respected him, but everyone knew that his health problems excluded him from assuming any additional responsibilities. Tregub took his usual seat in the third chair to the left of Arachev.

Then came Vladimir Gladskoi, one of the youngest Politburo members. Gladskoi was smart, disciplined and quietly confident. He had come up through the KGB, and was a handpicked Arachev protégé. He sat in the second chair from Arachev next to Tregub.

Finally, the ebullient Boris Gazin entered. Gazin emanated leadership. He could dominate most people by the sheer force of his personality. His fatal flaw was that he was a man ruled by his appetites—particularly his love for alcohol. His greatest redeeming quality was that he could be counted on when it was time to fight. That was when he was at his best. Both these strengths and weaknesses made Gazin perfectly suited for the leadership role that Arachev had in mind for him.

Arachev began the meeting. "Comrades, today's historic meeting will be remembered forever as a banner day in the march toward the Marxist New World Order. The time has come to take a very bold and courageous step into the final phase of our beloved world revolution. Gentlemen, allow me to layout the blueprint, as I see it, for the conclusion of the dreams of Marx, Engels and Lenin.

"All of us in this room have been privy to the marvelous advances of the world revolution. We have shared in the tremendous victories accomplished by our agents around the world—particularly in the West. They have gained control of the educational systems, the media, the clergy and, most recently, the corporate boardrooms. Of course, all of you are well aware of the extent to which we have been able to obtain control in most of the political parties, whether they are considered liberal or conservative.

"Most European nations have now embraced the socialist ideology and have elected socialist governments. These developments indicate that the time has come for the full realization of a world government established on the Marxist-Leninist ideals of socialism.

"Our ultimate victory is inevitable. Our masters of re-education have so effectively infiltrated the educational systems and the news services of the West, that they now espouse the very concepts of socialism while claiming to oppose them. However, that does not mean there are no obstacles yet to be surmounted."

"The biggest obstacle to the final realization of our world revolution is the latent fear of communism and of the Soviet Union. All of us understand the power of long-held beliefs and how difficult it can be to shake them. After all, we are the people who gave the world the lesson of Pavlov's dog.

"Therefore, I purpose three radical and daring steps. First of all, I purpose that we stage the dissolution of the Soviet Union. This will deprive the West of an enemy.

"Secondly, I purpose that we propagate the myth that capitalism and the West won the Cold War. We know that our agents now hold the reins of power in almost every nation of Europe, even as I speak. If that had not been true, we would never have allowed the fall of the Berlin Wall. Yet, it is vital that the Western world believe that the Marxist threat has been totally vanquished. All of us at this table know that the socialist bloc of nations can win any vote at the United Nations' General Assembly anytime we choose. It has been proven over and over. With the dissolution of the Soviet Union, we are trading three votes for fifteen. This will increase our margin of power in that body even more.

"Last, but not least, I purpose that we stage my overthrow as leader of the Soviet Union in order for my leadership to become acceptable on the global stage. That's where I need to be in order to affect the final conclusion of the revolution."

At this last proposal, a murmur of surprise passed among the Politburo members. Arachev had purposely not shared this part of his plan with any of the leadership. As he had anticipated, the daring of the staged coup captured the admiration of every man in the room.

Alexei Tregub felt that a word of caution was needed, "Comrade Arachev, these are bold and far-reaching steps you are proposing. While I admire your courage, what if they don't work? It is possible that we could lose the entire revolution."

Mikhail smiled. He and Rada had gone over this question hundreds of times now. "Comrade Tregub, I've asked myself the same question. However, every man at this table knows the truth. Socialism, as we have attempted it, has failed. We have sold the myth that the Soviet Union is a superpower, but all of us know that much of our country lives on a Third World level. Without drastic steps now, our revolution will face extinction."

Gladskoi dared to ask the obvious, "If socialism has failed so miserably, why should we even try to implement it on a global scale?"

"It's a fair question, Comrade," Arachev answered smoothly. "Socialism has not failed. Its improper implementation has failed. We know that capitalism, with its excesses and inequalities, is destined for defeat. As we speak, the West is ready to accept socialism in its new form. Some are even calling it neo-socialism. Under neo-socialism, ownership of the means of production will remain in the individual's hands rather than everything being owned by the state."

Tregub broke in, "But if private ownership is allowed, that's not socialism."

"Actually it is," Arachev explained. "Socialism is control of the means of production in an economy. When the government is able to take the cream off the profits through taxation and can control every aspect of a business through regulations and policies, the government is, in reality, controlling the means of production without the headaches of actual ownership."

Boris Gazin spoke up, "So that's the reason it's called neo-socialism. It is socialism, but coming in through the back door. It's brilliant! I'm all for it."

The news of Arachev's ouster rocked the world. The only person on earth who didn't seem too upset by it was Arachev himself. He was already busily working on creating conditions necessary for the final transition to a genuine New World Order.

Chapter Seven

While president of the Soviet Union, Michael had made many globalist friends in very high places. Already knowing where he intended to go, he had cultivated these friendships with great care.

One particularly important person was a Canadian named Morris Samuels. Samuels was a socialist billionaire, and was a globalist from the top of his head to the soles of his feet. At different times, Morris and Michael would stay up late into the night discussing the best path for the world to take as it progressed into the emerging global government.

It was during one of these midnight sessions that the key vehicle for the journey into world government was settled upon.

"We will never inspire the world to take the leap into world government without a cause," Morris flatly stated to Michael. "The masses have never been willing to march unless possessed with a cause."

"And do you have something in mind?" Michael inquired.

"Actually, I do," came Samuel's reply. "Michael, all nations are now interdependent. They all breathe the same air, and share the same water. The environment is an international problem. No nation, no matter how powerful, can deal with these environmental issues alone."

Michael immediately understood. "I see your point, Morris," he acknowledged. "International government can only become reality as national governments are willing to adopt and submit to international laws. Every type of human behavior affects the environment in one way or another. If we can convince the people of the world concerning the urgency of environmental problems, they can be pressured into acceptance of international laws and their enforcement."

Morris smiled with satisfaction. Then he warned, "The challenge will be selling this concept to the powerful nations of the world. You know how jealously some of them guard their national sovereignty—especially the United States. Furthermore, many of these environmental problems are a little hard to prove. A person has to take some of it on faith."

"Leave it to me," Michael responded immediately. "Persuasion is my specialty. I've been told that I could sell a freezer to an Eskimo in the heartland of Antarctica," Michael said with a slight grin. "We can activate our contacts in the media, launching a 'Save the Planet' campaign. Before long everyone will be recycling and adopting laws to save the ozone layer."

"With my powerful connections at the United Nations, we could plan a global environmental summit," Morris suggested. "We are sure to get total support from the environmentalists, the animal rights activists and the New Age crowd. This earth summit would give the media something to talk about for years on end."

Arachev continued, "Out of that meeting we could establish a permanent environmental organization that could then be used to lobby the governments of the world to support each new environmental treaty."

Michael slipped into bed that night with that warm feeling of satisfaction that he always got when he sensed a good plan was coming together.

Chapter Eight

A few months later, a note arrived from Morris Samuels. "The next time you're in the United States, stop by my ranch for a couple of days. It will do you good." It was signed–"Your friend, Morris."

A few weeks later Morris' limousine picked up Michael and Rada at the Denver Airport. When they arrived at the beautiful 10,000-acre ranch, Morris and his wife Barbara were waiting. "It's so wonderful to see you again Michael," Morris exclaimed. "Rada, meet my wife Barbara. Barbara, this is Rada and Michael Arachev whom I've told you so much about."

Barbara was radiant, "I'm so happy to finally meet both of you. Welcome to our little ranch. This is where we come to get away from it all."

Rada was immediately attracted to Barbara. There was something almost surreal about her. Rada couldn't quite put her finger on it, but she was definitely intrigued by this woman.

"Can we get you something to drink? Lemonade...ice tea?" Barbara inquired.

It was Michael who spoke up, "Not right now. I'm so anxious to see your ranch. Can we get the grand tour right away?"

"Certainly," Morris responded. Soon, one of the groundskeepers appeared with a golf cart large enough for the four of them. As they headed down the beautifully manicured lane, Michael could feel himself beginning to relax. "This is going to be a good two days," he thought.

The tour was more than Rada and Michael had bargained for. Ten thousand acres is a lot of land. Not far from the palatial Victorian home was the golf course. The course and the greens were landscaped meticulously.

Beyond the golf course was a 3,000-acre wildlife preserve. The trip through the reserve was incredibly relaxing. They saw deer, bear, a bobcat, a herd of buffalo—and every other kind of small wildlife imaginable.

After about two hours, they approached the end of the tour. Rada sensed that the Samuels were saving something special for last. Approaching the extreme southern part of the ranch, they emerged from the woods into what appeared to be a small village. Many people were moving leisurely about.

At this point, Barbara took charge. "We'll be walking for this part of the tour," she announced.

They first approached a small quaint temple. Over the entranceway was inscribed 'Ahura Mazda.' As they entered, they were greeted by a brilliant golden sunset painted on the western wall. In the middle of the room, a priest was tending to a fire. There were several worshipers standing at different places around the fire nodding and praying. Barbara explained, "This is a Zoroastrian temple. Zoroastrians believe there is one eternal God 'Ahura Mazda'. The founder of Zoroastrianism was the prophet, Zoroaster, meaning 'he of the golden light.' Zoroastrians must pray five times every day in the presence of fire. They take special care about the purity of fire, water and earth."

Leaving the Zoroastrian temple, they next approached a small but beautiful Jewish synagogue. Barbara explained to Michael and Rada, "King Solomon prayed a prayer at the dedication of Israel's First Temple. In this prayer, he requested that God would hear the prayers of

Jewish people everywhere if they would pray toward the site of the temple. Consequently, this synagogue and all other synagogues in the world are built so that the worshipers face toward the Temple Mount in Jerusalem."

Inside the synagogue, several Jews were praying. Each wore a prayer shawl and bobbed his head back and forth as he prayed.

As they left the synagogue, Barbara warned, "This next place of worship is a little different. We are getting ready to visit the Wiccans. The word Wicca means witch. But these people are perfectly harmless I can assure you."

They approached an open area in the shape of a circle that was decorated with many symbols. There was a large pentagram, a tapestry containing a half moon, a large broom, and several candelabra. At the north part of the circle, there was an altar. Barbara explained, "The Wiccans do not normally worship inside a building. They like to worship under the light of the moon."

Rada noticed the pentagram, in particular. "What is the meaning of that?" she inquired.

"The five points of the star correspond to the elements air, earth, fire and water with the top point corresponding to spirit," Barbara explained.

There was something about this Wiccan site that strangely pulled at Rada. She couldn't put her finger on it, but something was definitely there.

Barbara continued her explanation, "Many witches and Wiccans believe in some form of reincarnation and that the results, or karma, of past deeds can follow a person from one life to the next. This may also explain why terrible things sometimes happen to wonderful people, or why some people seem to have been born with certain skills and knowledge. It may also explain why some people seem to lead a 'charmed' life."

Michael listened carefully to all of the explanations. His attention was especially arrested when Barbara mentioned some people having a 'charmed' life. He had often wondered why so many breaks and opportunities seemed to come his way. "Is there a chance I might have had a former life?" he wondered to himself.

There were several other centers of worship in the village, but they didn't take time to visit them all. However, there was one more stop that Barbara insisted they make. She led them to the magnificent edifice in the center of the village. The inscription over the door read "Temple of Understanding."

"The reason I insisted that we come here," Barbara explained, "is because this is where everything comes together. As you know, religious conflict is the scourge of our world. If the world could accept what is taught here in the Temple of Understanding, all of these conflicts would cease."

"It's an intriguing name," Michael said. "But I've never heard of it before. Tell us about it."

"Well," Barbara replied, "the Temple of Understanding was founded in 1960 by Juliet Hollister. Its mission is to promote understanding among the world's religions, to recognize the oneness of the human family and to achieve a spiritual United Nations.

"Her idea came to the attention of Eleanor Roosevelt who immediately caught the vision. She wrote letters to influential people who could assist in the realization of the vision. The Temple of Understanding has become a leading advocate of Interfaithism and is an NGO (non-governmental organization) at the United Nations."

Michael quickly broke in, "I find it interesting that the Temple of Understanding envisions a spiritual United Nations, and that Eleanor Roosevelt was a leading advocate. I had a professor in college who taught us that President Franklin Roosevelt was the prime mover behind the formation of the political United Nations. Now you're telling me that his wife advocated forming a United Nations of religions!"

Morris broke in, "At the time the UN was formed, the Roosevelts understood the need for the world's religious thinking to be united. Because of the depth of religious animosity, this concept has not progressed as quickly as political union. However, momentum toward a global spirituality is building very rapidly now."

"So do you foresee the possibility of a United Nations of Religions actually being founded?" Michael asked intently.

"No doubt about it," Morris replied. "It's only a matter of time."

"Do you understand what this means, Morris?" Michael questioned excitedly. "Do you understand that the last huge obstacle to our New World Order can now be overcome?"

"Michael, that's exactly why Barbara and I have built this Interfaith village," Morris answered with considerable satisfaction.

Michael was now so interested that he said enthusiastically, "Let's take a look inside."

When they entered the Temple, Michael was totally amazed at what he saw. Jews, Zoroastrians, Hindus, Jains, Buddhists, Wiccans and many other worshipers were praying together in perfect harmony. Turning to Morris he exclaimed, "What you have accomplished here is simply wonderful!"

Morris quickly replied, "Don't give me the credit. Barbara has done almost everything in this village. She's the spiritual force in our family."

While in the Temple of Understanding, one thing in particular caught Michael's attention. On the north wall was a large inscription–"Our Environment is a Religious Issue." Michael turned to Barbara and asked, "Do these people believe that the environment is a religious issue?"

"Oh, yes," Barbara replied quickly. "All of these religions have three things in common. They revere nature, they do not try to convert others and they do not believe that their religion is the only valid religion."

On the way back to the house, Michael had one question burning in the back of his mind. He finally blurted out what was bothering him. "What about Christians? How do they fit into this scenario? They're too great in number to be ignored."

Morris was the one who answered, "Actually, that's not as much of a problem as it may seem. The environmental agenda is being embraced more and more by mainstream Christianity."

Barbara broke in, "And the ecumenical movement has, to a great extent, brought a halt to Christian efforts to convert people of other Christian denominations. That's the case with the exception of certain fundamentalist Christian groups. Those will eventually join the mainstream, or they will become increasingly marginalized."

Rada spoke up, "But I thought Christianity was an exclusive religion. Didn't Jesus teach that He was the only Savior and thus the only way to salvation?"

"Well, historically that has been true," Barbara agreed. "However, there are great changes taking place in Christianity. The largest sector of Christianity, Roman Catholicism, is taking the lead in this regard. They recently published a new catechism, which states that people do not have to believe Jesus was the Messiah in order to be included in the plan of salvation."

"You have to be kidding me!" Michael said excitedly.

"Oh no," Barbara replied. "Article No. 841 in the catechism addresses the church's relationship with the Muslims. It says, 'The plan of salvation also includes those who acknowledge the Creator, in the first place amongst whom are the Muslims; these profess to hold the faith of Abraham, and together with us they adore the one, merciful God, mankind's judge on the last day.'"

"And other mainstream Christian denominations are following suit," Morris added. "Some Christian groups probably will not compromise, but they are in the minority. When our New World Order is securely in place, we will find a way to deal with them."

As Michael lay in bed that night, his mind raced with excitement. He said to Rada, "Once people acknowledge that there is no absolute truth, then they can be led to believe most anything. We are much further along toward the realization of a global spirituality than I thought possible."

Rada smiled at Michael's enthusiasm. "Why should that surprise you? When something is predestined, the pieces seem to mysteriously fit together."

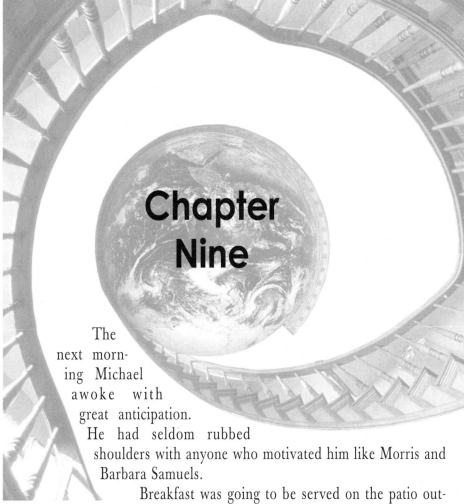

Chapter Nine

The next morning Michael awoke with great anticipation. He had seldom rubbed shoulders with anyone who motivated him like Morris and Barbara Samuels.

Breakfast was going to be served on the patio outside the sitting room. The weather was a perfect 73 degrees. The patio furniture was white wicker with soft green cushions and flowered green tablecloths. While breakfast was being prepared, Morris inquired, "Well Michael, what do you want to do today?"

There was no hesitation in Michael's reply, "I want the four of us to lay plans for the 'Save the Earth Summit' we discussed yesterday. I don't think we have any time to waste."

"That's fine by me," Morris agreed, "as long as the women don't have plans to go shopping instead."

"If Rada has a choice between shopping and discussing the future of the world, she'll choose global planning every time," Michael assured him laughingly.

Morris smiled. "It sounds like we married the same kind of women. Those are Barbara's feelings exactly."

The breakfast was fixed to perfection, as was everything that the Samuels had anything to do with. As the four of them ate, it was obvious that the camaraderie of the previous day was still flowing among them. Morris and Michael informed their wives about what they had in mind for the day. Rada and Barbara were excited at the prospect of such a stimulating challenge.

Morris sent word to his secretary that she would be needed in 10 minutes. He wanted to be sure that all ideas were properly recorded for future use. He requested that coffee, tea and soft drinks be available in the sitting room where the brainstorming was to take place.

Michael opened the conversation. "Morris, you intimated yesterday that actions taken at an Earth Summit could end up becoming international law. I know you are one of the foremost experts in the world on the United Nations and international law. Exactly how that would work?"

Morris began, "As all of you know, a system of international law was envisioned when the United Nations was formed in 1945. International law is formed by the adoption of international treaties. When a treaty is negotiated and signed between governments, the treaty becomes what we call 'soft law.' It is generally agreed that each government will respect what has been signed while awaiting the ratification of the treaty by its parliament or congress."

Morris continued his explanation, "Once the treaty is ratified by the nation's parliament, the provisions of the treaty then become what we call 'hard law.' Nations are then obligated to adhere to those laws as faithfully as they would expect their citizens to obey their own national laws."

"And if they don't, then what?" Rada asked.

"Well, that's been the weakness in the system up until now," Morris replied. "However, slowly but surely, mechanisms have been created to put teeth into international law so we can have a truly functioning system of global governance."

"And how is that being accomplished?" Michael inquired.

"There are several different things that must be understood," Morris explained. "In the case of very serious violations of international law, which could threaten world peace, actions can be taken by the UN Security Council, as you know. These actions may take the form of placing a nation under economic sanctions. In this case, all UN members are obligated by the UN Charter to boycott the offending nation economically. Normally, the threat of economic sanctions has been enough to bring the disobedient nation into compliance with international law."

"But Morris," Barbara interrupted, "haven't there been some cases where this didn't work—where nations continued to resist the will of the UN, even after being sanctioned economically? What happens in those cases?"

"In those cases, the UN Security Council may vote to take military action against that nation. The 1991 UN action against Iraq and Saddam Hussein is a recent case in point."

"But hasn't the effectiveness of this system been limited by the 'Big Five' nations that have veto power over the decisions of the Security Council?" Rada inquired.

"Veto power has been the big flaw in this system," Morris agreed. "Not only have the 'Big Five' wielded that power to protect themselves against Security Council action, but also they have used it to protect their allies from the enforcement power of the UN."

"Then, is it reasonable to expect compliance with environmental treaties?" Michael asked.

"Probably not," Morris admitted, "if we continue to operate as we have in the past. However, there are important developments on the horizon. From as early as 1948, there have been plans on the drawing board to create a court system at the global level, which could enforce the edicts of the United Nations and international law. However, resistance to any infringement on national sovereignty has been so intense, that progress toward a world court system has not been possible, until recently.

"As the world's nations have begun to think more globally, the idea of a court system at the world level has received a much greater degree of acceptance. It now appears that a world court could be a reality within the next few years. Once this comes to pass, international law will be enforceable, not only upon nations, but also upon individual citizens."

Rada inquired with intense interest, "Are you saying that we are nearing the time when individual citizens could be prosecuted for the violation of world law by a world court system?"

"Definitely," Morris affirmed.

"This would finally put the necessary teeth into world government!" Michael exclaimed with enthusiasm. "It's exactly what we need."

"Yes, but it would not be wise to discuss this in a public forum at this time," Morris warned. "We might sabotage the idea before it has a chance to get off the ground. I'm sure all of us in this room can appreciate that fact."

"Now that we all understand the workings of international law and how it will be enforced in the future, let's dive into planning the Save the Earth Summit," Barbara said excitedly.

"I always like to define the goal first," Michael interjected. "Let's state what it is that we are trying to accomplish."

Rada cut to the chase. "Our stated purpose will be to save the world from global warming, polluted water and contaminated air. The goal, as stated for public consumption, will be 'to save mankind from environmental disaster while there is still time'."

"However," she continued, "our real goal is to form a world government founded on the principles of democratic socialism. The environmental movement we hope to foster is simply a means to an end."

Morris smiled at her candor. "Rada," he said, "this room is one of the few places in the world that you could make that statement without creating an anti-world government revolution. If certain elements of the press heard Michael Arachev's wife speaking openly of intentions to create a world government, our program would be set back by fifty years. All of us must be very discreet about what we say and to whom we speak. It will be the best policy to never refer to our plan as a world government—although we all know very well that's exactly what it is. There are still large groups out there that have a knee-jerk reaction against the term 'world government.' The politically correct phrase that we will use from now on will be 'global governance'."

"But Morris," Rada protested. "Do you think a slight change in wording could make that much difference? Let's face it—it's only a matter of semantics."

"I know Rada," Morris replied patiently. "But when leading the masses, perception is everything. Patriotism is one of the most deeply held emotions in the heart of mankind. People will proudly send their sons and their husbands to die in a war that they don't even understand, all for the love of their country. Nationalism is a cancer on the human soul, but it is so deeply embedded in the human psyche that we will have to be very careful as we slowly but surely erode it."

Michael broke back into the conversation. "I've found that, if programs are to succeed in moving the masses, they must be kept very simple. I believe this will be imperative as we launch the final phase of our plan."

"The key will be to focus on two or three concepts, and to pound away at them relentlessly," Barbara added. "We will need to enlist every journalist and every newscaster sympathetic to our cause to help sell our message, which will have to be clearly defined."

As an avid environmentalist, Rada chimed in, "First of all, you have global warming caused by man putting unacceptably high levels of carbon dioxide into the air. Scientists contend that, if this is not corrected in the next fifteen to twenty years, the damage to the earth's atmosphere will be irreversible. The environmentalists have already assembled a mighty army to fight against carbon dioxide emissions, and I'm sure they would gladly join us in the fight."

"But Rada, people have been questioning whether or not global warming is real," Barbara challenged. "It would be a tragedy to build an entire movement around something that could possibly end up being discredited."

"Barbara, it doesn't matter whether it's true or not," Rada replied matter-of-factly. "The scientists, who say it is true, can't prove it right now—though they claim to have strong arguments. On the other hand, their detractors can't prove that it's not happening. Since we don't know for sure, we will act as though it is true. If we wait until we have absolute proof, it could be too late to save the earth. Furthermore, if it is proven to be untrue in 2025, what will it matter? Our New World Order will be in total control by then. The important thing is that global warming can be used to force world leaders to accept the implementation and enforcement of international law."

"Barbara, do you see why I quit debating with Rada years ago?" Michael quipped with a smile.

"Actually, she's convinced me," Barbara laughed.

"I think the second plank in our platform must be global poverty," Morris stated with obvious conviction. "How any world leader can sleep at night, knowing that half of the world's inhabitants are existing on less than $2 per day, is beyond me. Furthermore, it's the epitome of injustice when twenty percent of the world's population consumes eighty percent of the world's natural resources. This unconscionable situation demands unified action by the nations of the world. Leaders of capitalistic nations know that wealth redistribution has been the number one plank in the platform of international communism for many years, so we may have to promote this program by another name."

Barbara broke in. "I've got it!" she exclaimed. "Let's call it the 'War on Poverty.' Who in their right mind would want to oppose fighting against poverty with all of its accompanying ills?"

"I think it will work," Michael stated with satisfaction. "We have come up with two very powerful issues that will motivate many people.

"There is one other thing we should never forget," Michael added. "My experience in the Soviet Union taught me that once we start moving toward our goals, world events have a way of dumping issues in our laps that may be more powerful than the ones we have conceived. When this happens, we must be prepared to quickly adopt those issues as our own and ride them to victory."

"What is our timetable?" Morris asked. "I think we'll need a year to plan."

In his usual impetuous way, Michael said, "Well, what are we waiting for? Let's begin!"

Chapter Ten

After Michael had set in motion the plans for the Save the Earth Summit, he turned his attention in another direction.

There were not many forces on the earth with the potential to block his plan for one-world government...but there were a few. Michael felt he had to make sure that each of these forces was either in his corner or neutralized.

The number one power that concerned him was the Roman Catholic Church. You simply couldn't ignore a movement that represented and controlled the thinking of one billion of the world's inhabitants. Furthermore, its center of influence still resided in Europe, the same Europe that served as the seat of the Holy Roman Empire for the last 1,000 years. Now the states of Europe had joined themselves together as the European Union, which would soon be a virtual United States of Europe with nearly 500 million citizens, a common currency and a European president.

Most people had no idea how powerful the church could be. But Arachev knew firsthand that the Roman Church had the finest diplomatic network of any power on earth. Its tentacles of information extended into virtually every nation, state, county, parish, and neighborhood in the world. And information is power.

The question he had to answer was—where would the Church stand as the New World Order came together? How doctrinaire would it be? How much would the Church be willing to compromise in order to share in the power of the coming global system?

Arachev understood that only one person could speak for the Roman Church with absolute authority. Although the Pope's claim to infallibility was regularly criticized in many quarters, Michael had to admit that things were certainly simplified when one man led a nation or religious entity with undisputed power.

Arachev summoned Nikolai Tubolsk, his personal assistant, to his office. "Nikolai, please arrange a visit with Pope Paul VII at the earliest possible date," Arachev instructed.

"Sir, the Pope's staff will want to know the purpose of the meeting so that His Holiness can be properly prepared. What should I tell them?" Nikolai inquired.

"Simply tell the Pope that I want to continue the work we began together when I was president of the Soviet Union. He'll be glad to see me," Arachev assured.

Michael smiled to himself as his memory recycled the events of the first encounter with Pope Paul VII. It was a rare occasion indeed when two true global thinkers met face to face. The instant chemistry between Arachev and Paul VII had been unmistakable. They discussed the end of the Cold War and the unprecedented opportunities that this juncture in history presented for mankind.

Now Arachev felt the time had arrived for a more complete discussion concerning the role of the Catholic Church in his envisioned New World Order.

As the limousine made its way slowly through the streets of Rome, Michael and Rada's eyes drank in the historic landmarks that permeated the City of Seven Hills. Michael thought of all the world leaders before him who had made their way to the Vatican. He remembered Stalin's impudent question when it was suggested that the Pope be consulted concerning the future of Europe. "The Pope? How many divisions can he put on the battlefield?" Stalin had asked derisively. Yet Stalin was now dead and repudiated, and the papacy lived on.

Michael mused to himself, "What is it about the Vatican that ultimately compels every world leader to come calling?" Why was he coming? It wasn't because he believed in God.

The answer was simple. He was here because of power. The Vatican was one of the major power centers of the world.

As Michael and Rada stepped from the limousine, Michael's eyes swept over the Swiss guards standing at attention. As though on cue, Vatican Secretary of State, Agnola Calogera, came forward to welcome them, and to escort them to their audience with Pope Paul VII. Even though Michael had been welcomed as a head-of-state many times throughout the capitals of the world, he could not help but be impressed by the unerring adherence to protocol by the Vatican and by the knowledge that world leaders had been coming here for the last 1,200 years. Every single aspect of the reception was designed to convey the message that you were soon to be ushered into the presence of the most powerful and important person on earth.

As they approached the inner sanctum of the Pope's living quarters, the doormen and the Pope's personal attendants all stood silently in their proper places.

Pope Paul VII welcomed the Arachevs and their aides in the parlor. Then Michael and the Pope withdrew to the adjoining study where their discussions were to be held.

When alone, the Pope spoke warmly, "Michael!" the Pope exclaimed. "What a pleasure to see you again."

"It's my honor, Your Holiness," Arachev replied.

It was obvious that the meeting had been meticulously prepared. Documents were laid out on the working table, undoubtedly pertaining to the subjects that Arachev had indicated he wanted to discuss.

Michael immediately moved to the object of his visit. "Your Holiness, world events have moved very rapidly since we last met. With each passing day, nations are becoming increasingly interdependent. I'm sure you recall our discussion concerning the emerging New World Order."

Pope Paul VII nodded as Michael spoke. "I remember very well. It is as though it were yesterday."

Michael continued, choosing his words very carefully, "It seems to me we have entered the endgame in the alignment of global powers that will preside over the coming new age of which we dream. Your insight and counsel at this pivotal time would be invaluable to those of us working for a future of peace and security."

"Michael," the Pope began, "it is vital that we understand what must be done in order to create the proper structures of global governance. And I think it's too late in the game to dance around the critical issues.

"First of all, we must identify, in no uncertain terms, the root causes of conflict in our world. Nationalism has plunged the world repeatedly into war. We must face the truth. The day of the nation-state is over. We have truly entered a new age—the age of globalism."

Arachev nodded appreciatively. This was going much better than he had thought possible. It surprised him that Pope Paul VII was advocating one-world government so openly. What he didn't know was that the Pope had been keeping an exhaustive file on him for many years. The text of every speech he had made and every person with whom he had met for the last 10 years was catalogued in meticulous detail in the files of the Vatican. The Pope knew that he was an avid proponent of world government. He also knew that Arachev was the most likely candidate to become the political leader of that world government. Furthermore, the Pope understood that Arachev had come to explore whether forming an alliance with his church was possible. Pope Paul VII had already concluded that such an alliance was not only possible, but necessary.

Michael proceeded boldly, "Your Holiness, are you saying that the church would favor the establishment of a system of world government?"

"It is the only answer, given present realities," the Pope replied immediately. "The church has been a believer in global government for a long time.

"Way back in the '50's, Pope Pius XII spoke of the necessity of a supranational world order. He declared that 'Catholics...above all...must realize that they are called to overcome every vestige of nationalistic narrowness...'

"Our beloved Pope John XXIII, in his encyclical 'Peace on Earth,' written in the early 1960's, called for the strengthening of the United Nations, giving it worldwide power so that it would be able to work for the universal common good. John XXIII stated that 'such a government must be founded because all nations are now interdependent.'

"Pierre Boillon, the late bishop of Verdun, France, stated the position of the church most clearly. Speaking concerning internationalism, Boillon said, 'Therefore we must emphasize the great moral responsibility to empower an international authority to prevent war. The entire world must become aware that if this institution is to become effective, every nation must renounce its ultimate sovereignty to this universal authority. This is an obligation! If nations, if rulers of nations, if public opinion will not accept this renunciation, then they really are voting for war, however beautiful may be their speeches on peace'."

Michael's mind raced as he attempted to assimilate all of this stunning information, and to determine the implications for the world's future. It certainly looked like this was a religion with which he could do business!

He wanted to reaffirm all the Pope had said to him. "So the Church's position is not only that a system of world government would be desirable, but that it is an absolute necessity for the continued evolution of human history?" he asked.

Pope Paul VII nodded in vigorous assent. "We have no choice. Technological advances have created a global village in which all nations are now interdependent. Environmental problems cannot be solved by nations independently. The current of history is actually imposing upon us the necessity of creating new forms of global governance."

"Exactly," Arachev agreed. "We couldn't be in more perfect agreement on these issues.

"There is one more sensitive subject I must discuss with you, Your Holiness," Michael ventured. "We have recently emerged from the Cold War. Yet, there are still many disagreements concerning the economic system that will rule our New World Order. What is the feeling of the Church on this?"

The Pope weighed his words carefully. "The Church does not always follow the latest political or economic fad that comes along. We believe God chooses those He wants to lead His church and that the sheep should follow. We are much more comfortable with established authority providing leadership, and, frankly, we think it is a more Christian way."

"Would the Church favor socialism over capitalism as an economic form?" Michael inquired anxiously.

The Pope smiled. "I see you haven't read the speech I gave before the United Nations. Before all the nations of the world, I called for massive wealth redistribution."

A socialist from birth, Michael knew that wealth redistribution was the central plank in the platform of international communism. When the full realization of what the Pope was saying dawned on Michael, a broad smile spread across his face. He rose to his feet, shaking hands with Pope Paul VII warmly. "So we are partners in this historic task of leading mankind into the emerging era of globalism!" Michael declared excitedly.

The Pope vigorously returned the handshake, nodding his agreement.

As the two men parted, they both understood that one overriding question remained untouched and unanswered. When the New World Order was finally established in all of its power, who would wield ultimate authority—the political leader or the spiritual leader?

Chapter Eleven

A few months later, a discreet inquiry arrived at Arachev's headquarters from the leading caliph of the Muslim world. "Perhaps the time has arrived for us to sit down together," the hand-delivered message simply said.

As the advance of globalization gained momentum, it became obvious to all potential players on the geopolitical chessboard that they must cement alliances in order to play a meaningful role in the emerging New World Order.

Imam Khaled al-Hassan had carefully observed the meeting between Arachev and Pope Paul VII with no small apprehension. He understood what a formidable force an alliance between the world's dominant political powers and the Roman Church would be. It would not bode well for the future of the Muslim world if Islam were left on the outside looking in.

The meeting between Arachev and the Imam was held in absolute secrecy in Geneva, Switzerland. The Muslims felt that neutrality was important for this meeting. The UN Secretary General graciously provided meeting facilities at one of the UN complexes located about 20 miles outside Geneva's city limits.

As usual, Arachev, his wife Rada, and his staff arrived several days early in order to prepare for this critical summit. Any meeting with the leader of 1.2 billion human beings had to be approached with the utmost seriousness and care. One thing was certain. If Muslims were to play a meaningful role in the New World Order, they would have to accept the inclusive global spirituality that would allow all religions to co-exist in peace and mutual respect.

The Imam and his entourage arrived at the UN villa at 12:45 p.m. As Michael and Rada prepared to receive them, they were informed that the Muslim prayer time was to begin in 10 minutes.

"How long will that last?" Michael asked.

"The afternoon prayer lasts for thirty minutes," the Imam's secretary explained.

A brief shadow of irritation passed across Arachev's face. Michael quickly regained his composure. "I should have remembered that the prayer times would have to be allowed for. Everyone knows Muslims pray five times a day," he mentally chastised himself.

Imam al-Hassan was taken straight to the East Room. This room had been specifically prepared to accommodate the Muslim prayers since it was located on the extreme eastern side of the building, with windows entirely along that side. This allowed the worshipers to face Mecca during their prayers.

Once the Imam and his disciples were settled into their prayer routine, Arachev used the excuse of visiting the restroom in order to observe the Muslim devotions. He watched as the Islamic delegation knelt looking to the east. Then they bowed their foreheads to the ground for a period of time. After this, they came back to their knees and then stood up, still oblivious to anything going on around them. Just when it seemed that the prayers were probably over, the entire routine started all over again.

Michael was deep in thought as he continued down the hall. This was the closest he had ever been to people of this level of spiritual devotion. Something about the Muslim prayer ritual was unsettling. How could you deal with people on an intellectual basis who were so steeped in medieval beliefs? On the other hand, if they could follow this mystical Prophet Mohammed, with all of his apparent contradictions, Michael felt sure he could persuade them to follow him.

After the prayers finished, the UN facilitator who coordinated activities at the villa ushered the Imam and his staff into the conference room. The formal introductions were made, and the usual polite pleasantries were exchanged.

Arachev then steered the discourse straight to his purpose. "Your honor," he began, nodding toward the Imam, "and distinguished guests. I appreciate this opportunity to meet with you.

"As you know, our world finds itself standing at the crossroads of history. Globalization and the increasing interdependency of nations have mandated the emergence of a new order. This is happening whether we like it or not.

"What is within our power is the ability to determine whether this New World Order will usher in a new era of hope with peace and security, or whether it will bring to the human race deepening conflicts and wars that very likely could result in the extinction of mankind itself."

Warming to his subject, Michael continued, "We all realize that, historically, the most divisive force on earth has been religion. Most of history's wars have been the result of conflicting religious beliefs that finally pulled the adherents into armed struggle.

"The same religious conflicts exist today, but now there is a huge difference. Our world possesses weapons of mass destruction. If we continue to allow religious differences to foster division and conflict among the people of the earth, eventually a war will erupt that will spin out of control and destroy us all. The question is not if it will happen. The only question is when."

Imam al-Hassan rose to his feet at the end of the table. He paused for quite some time before speaking. "Mr. Arachev, your words are filled with wisdom, and we welcome them."

Michael breathed a silent sigh of relief. He didn't know how his ideas were being received by the practitioners of this Eastern religion called Islam.

The Imam continued, "We all know that the tides of history ebb and flow. They sweep away before them all that resist their will, and they will lead mankind to its ultimate destiny. An example of this was when our own Prophet Mohammed (Peace be upon him) was given to the world by the will of Allah, the one true God.

"In inexplicable fashion, the religion of Islam grew from one man, Mohammed, to the greatest force on the face of the earth. Today, 1.2 billion people embrace the Islamic faith. More people now give adherence to the teachings of Mohammed than profess allegiance to any other religion on earth.

"Any New World Order that does not recognize the central role that Islam must play is destined to failure. Seeing that Islam began from nothing in the early 7th Century to become the world's greatest religion today, it is obvious that the message of Islam is destined to provide light to the world as we move from the era of the nation-state into the time of global government."

Arachev decided it was time to cut to the heart of the matter. "Imam al-Hassan," he reasoned, "there are literally thousands of religions in the world today. To think that all of them could be merged into one religion is simply a fantasy. However, I do think there is a way to bring about unity among the major religions while still respecting diversity."

The Imam interrupted, "I don't see how such a thing could happen. Please explain."

Michael continued, "A sister organization to the United Nations called the United Religions has been envisioned. You know how separated the nations of the world were before the creation of the UN in 1945. Now, after less than half a century of effort, the nations of the world have been forged into the World Community, and, except for a few rogue states, we speak with a common voice. We believe the same can be accomplished with the religions of the world."

Imam al-Hassan replied carefully, "Islam is a religion of peace. It is also a religion of truth. The core truth that has brought light to one-fifth of the world's citizens is belief in only one God, Allah, and in the revelations given to Allah's Prophet Mohammed. When the world acknowledges this wonderful revelation, the enlightenment of mankind will have, in fact, arrived."

It began to dawn on Arachev that this wasn't going to be easy. But he decided to try again. With his warmest smile, he looked the Imam straight in the face, "I think perhaps I need for you to explain some things to me. I hear you say that yours is a religion of peace, yet in the name of Islam, violence is being perpetrated around the globe. How do you explain this?"

It was obvious that Imam Khaled al-Hassan had been asked this same question many, many times. The reply came without hesitation, "We do not approve of terrorism in any form. Those who commit terrorism in the name of Islam are, in reality, the enemies of Islam."

Michael broke in, "So, you do not condone the suicide bombings in Israel? I read that these 'martyrs' for the cause of Allah are promised immediate paradise."

"We must understand the definition of terrorism," the Imam replied. "When an enemy has taken your land and you are in a war of liberation, that is not considered terrorism."

"Even if the bombings target innocent women and children?" Arachev asked incredulously.

"There are no innocent women and children in this case," Imam al-Hassan contended. "These women have sons who grow up to enforce the occupation. In a few years these children will be flying the planes and driving the tanks used against the national aspirations of our brothers in Palestine."

Arachev's exasperation was starting to rise to the surface. He addressed the Islamic delegation more forcefully now, "The whole world knows the Muslims are not going to convert to Christianity. Likewise, the world's one billion Christians are not going to convert to the faith of Islam. Besides Christians and Muslims, there are the Hindus, the Zorastrians, the Bahai's and on and on. A thousand years from now there will still be different religions on the earth. This is simply a fact of life, whether we agree with it or not.

"Since this is true, we must deal with that reality. How do we prevent a world-engulfing holocaust that could come as early as today?

"We, who are attempting to build a better and safer world, think there is an answer. We simply can no longer tolerate religious conflict. Most major religions believe in one god. Some call Him Brahma, some Jehovah, some Jesus and others Allah. Why can't we simply agree that we are all referring to the same God, even though we know Him by different names? The time has come for all people to denounce religious conflict, to renounce the practice of proselytizing and to teach their children to accept and respect diversity in religious thought and practice."

The Imam cleared his throat. "If you are asking us to recognize the legitimacy of pagan forms of religion, that will be impossible," he said emphatically. "We would have to renounce the teachings of Prophet Mohammed to adopt such a belief. The cornerstone of all truth in the universe is that there is one God, Allah, and that Mohammed is his prophet. Belief and submission to this truth is the key to peace on earth."

"But Imam al-Hassan," Arachev protested, "you and I both know that such uniformity of belief is simply impossible! Humankind will plunge into the abyss of World War III before such a pipedream ever comes to pass."

Arachev decided to try one more approach. "How do you believe, in this world possessing weapons of mass destruction, the human race can avoid the global holocaust that seems all but inevitable?"

"The will of Allah will ultimately be done. We have no doubt about that," the Imam replied matter-of-factly. "Our Koran teaches us that the Al Mahdi will soon come to save humankind and usher in a Muslim world government. If we do not achieve peace before, we will realize it when the Mahdi comes."

"According to your prophets, what will the Mahdi do when he comes?" Arachev asked with more than a little interest.

"Mohammed told us what he will do," the Imam replied. "First of all, he will be a descendent of the Prophet. He will fill the earth with justice as it is now filled with injustice and tyranny. And he will rule the world for seven years."

It became obvious to the Imam that the encounter had reached an impasse. "Mr. Arachev," he said, "it is almost time for our evening prayers. Thank you for meeting with me. Perhaps we can meet again at some future date. Be assured that Islam will continue to work for peace on earth." With that, the entire Muslim delegation filed down the hall toward the East Room to pray.

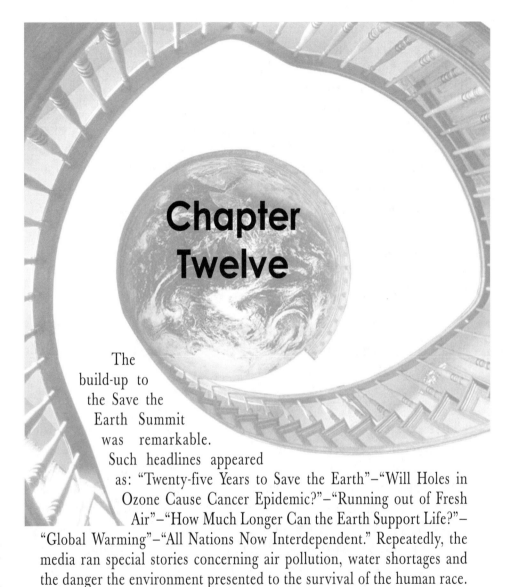

Chapter Twelve

The build-up to the Save the Earth Summit was remarkable. Such headlines appeared as: "Twenty-five Years to Save the Earth"–"Will Holes in Ozone Cause Cancer Epidemic?"–"Running out of Fresh Air"–"How Much Longer Can the Earth Support Life?"– "Global Warming"–"All Nations Now Interdependent." Repeatedly, the media ran special stories concerning air pollution, water shortages and the danger the environment presented to the survival of the human race. Suddenly, environmental issues were front-page news.

In all of this pre-summit hype, one message came through loud and clear: The environment is a global issue. No nation can face this life-threatening problem alone. We must now face these issues together or perish! All nations are now interdependent. We all breathe the same air. We all drink the same water. And we all have to live on the same earth.

Representatives from almost every nation attended the summit, including over 100 heads-of-state. The Rainbow Coalition was there. Environmentalists and animal rights activists sat in the front row. It was the world's environmental wakeup call.

An entire year of intense work had been put into preparation for the Save the Earth Summit. World-changing decisions almost never took place at a summit like this. The vital decisions were made during the preparatory meetings. Summits were simply to rally the foot soldiers and mobilize world opinion.

Since the purpose of this summit was to set the agenda for the 21st century, it was decided that the document to be sent home with all summit participants would be called Agenda 21. It was hoped that this document would become the roadmap for the world as it entered the new century.

When Michael Arachev strode to the podium for his keynote address, the convention hall fell silent. "Ladies and gentlemen, world leaders and fellow world citizens: We stand today at a defining moment for each of us and for our world. As melodramatic as it may sound, the future of our world is literally at stake at this time–the future of your homeland and mine, the future of our children and grandchildren, the future of our common home, Mother Earth.

"If we do not act now, our planet will become uninhabitable. As I speak to you, carbon dioxide emissions are eating away at the ozone layer that protects us all. The earth's vital resources are being consumed at an unacceptable rate. In the name of progress, industrial growth is advancing at an unsustainable pace.

"Ladies and gentlemen, this problem is not going to fix itself! The world community must now band together to save the common home we share. No nation can do it alone. We can no longer render mere lip service to caring for our environment. The time has come when we must make environmental reform our top priority!

"How can we remain passive when eighty percent of our world's resources are being consumed by twenty percent of the world's population? How can we rest when fifty percent of our earth's inhabitants exist on less than $2 per day? Can we expect the poor nations of the world to be content while the industrialized nations continue to exploit them? How can we expect to enjoy peace on earth when such inequity reigns?"

As Arachev spoke, you could feel the rising indignation from representatives of the Third World countries. Those from the Western world sat in uncomfortable silence.

Michael continued, "I am not suggesting today that we all return to the Stone Age. But there is a better alternative. We can do better! The time has come for us to demand that development be sustainable. Sustainable development simply requires that every action of man must take into account its effect on the earth and its environment. This is not an option. It is a necessity!

"We cannot continue raping our earth and expect it to survive! Now is the time to make the hard decisions necessary for our future existence. To do anything less is the height of irresponsibility and borders on being criminal."

Rada stole a sidelong glance at the President of the United States. His expression was impassive. The U.S., as the world's number one polluter, had the most to lose from this conference and the emerging environmental movement. Rada swung her attention back to her husband.

"So what must we do?" Arachev asked, his eyes moving from one world leader to the next. "We have prepared Agenda 21—a blueprint to halt and reverse environmental damage to our planet, and to promote environmentally sound and sustainable development in all countries on earth.

"For the far-reaching programs of Agenda 21 to be successful, a concern for the environment must begin to be integrated into every human action and every personal decision. What we manufacture, what we buy, what we wear, how we travel, what we eat, whom we choose as leaders; these and a myriad of other daily questions must begin to be answered with a recognition that every single human action has an impact upon both the environment and all other people.

"Is the challenge at hand a big one? It is huge! Is it impossible? No. If we are willing to give environmental issues the priority they deserve, we can still save this planet and restore it to health and sustainability. We can do it! Let us not be faint-hearted. Let us bring the human race together as never before to face the crisis at hand. We are one people. We share one environment. And we live in one common home. We must care for it. We must preserve it. Let's do it together!"

When Arachev finished speaking, the audience spontaneously rose to its feet. The clapping continued for nearly five minutes. Some in the crowd were actually seen wiping tears from their eyes. Here was hope. Here was the kind of leadership they had been yearning for–leadership not afraid to rally the people into making the hard sacrifices–leadership not afraid to challenge the big powers and hold them accountable. Even the President of the United States stood.

Chapter Thirteen

The Save the Earth Summit was a tremendous success. The morning after the close of the summit, Michael and Rada Arachev and Morris and Barbara Samuels met with Bhutto Mugavo, the Secretary General of the UN. He was all smiles.

"Smashing success!" Mugavo exclaimed as he entered the room. "All the major newspapers of the world are carrying stories about the summit today. Global awareness of environmental issues has never been this high! It is wonderful!"

The Secretary General continued, "I guess the next question is: Where do we go from here?"

Morris cleared his throat. "Actually, the answer to that question is more important than anything that happened at this summit. All of this hype will be gone in a few days. You don't change the course of the whole world with one summit, no matter how successful. The real key is relentless, grinding follow-through."

Michael interjected, "The critical thing, as I see it, is to employ full-time staffers accountable for implementing the actions of the summit." Looking at the Secretary General, he inquired, "Do you have a department available that would be able to assume responsibility for following up on decisions that have been made?"

Morris, being the UN expert that he was, chimed in, "The first thing we should do is establish a high-level Commission on Sustainable Development. This commission would report to the UN Economic and Social Council. This would ensure that the initiatives of the Save the Earth Summit are being carried out, and that UN agencies around the world are implementing the principles of sustainable development."

"Can the Economic and Social Council handle the additional workload?" Michael asked, turning to the Secretary General.

"Oh, I think so," Mugavo replied. "If we have to, we'll increase their budget in order to meet the need. This simply must be given first priority."

"Let's set our priorities right now," Michael said excitedly.

"I jotted a few things down during the summit that I thought would be important," Rada volunteered. Michael was not at all surprised. This was where Rada shined. He was the salesman, but she was the organizer behind the scenes.

"So what do you have?" Morris inquired.

"None of this will happen if it is left to chance. We must move to incorporate the decisions made at the summit into law," Rada declared.

"But how do you intend to do that?" The Secretary General was curious.

Rada explained, "We must devise treaties for nations to sign that will obligate them to carry out the goals set by the Save the Earth Summit."

"Do you think you can get them to sign?" Mugavo asked.

Rada smiled. "What did you think of the news coverage and the public pressure that brought over one hundred heads-of-state to our summit? You know that many of them did not want to be here, but public pressure forced them to come. The same approach will work for this."

Morris chimed in, "Once the treaties are signed, we will chip away little by little until we convince the parliaments to ratify. That accomplished, we will have brought the provisions of these treaties to the level of international law."

"But we still have a problem," Mugavo interjected. "Believe me. Just because you have international law, it doesn't mean the nations will obey. They only obey what they choose to obey."

"That brings us to my next point," Rada interjected. "We must have a World Court. Those who violate international law will be held accountable to the World Court."

"And you think you can accomplish that?" the Secretary General asked incredulously.

"You wait and see," Michael admonished. "You just wait and see."

"One more thing," Rada said. "And this may be the most important. We must stay on message. The key phrase is 'sustainable development.' This concept provides the rationale for every action we want to take, for every treaty that will need to be signed. The rulers of nations will accept more encroachment upon their national sovereignties under the guise of sustainable development than we might think possible."

Barbara, who hadn't said much, joined in. "I think Rada's last point of continually talking about sustainable development is critical. We all want development, but we don't want development that is going to ultimately destroy our world. It makes sense, and it feels right. The world will accept controls if they are made to believe they are essential to sustainable development."

Everyone nodded in agreement. Sustainable development was definitely a horse that they could ride.

Michael pulled his chair closer to the others in the room. "As we leave the summit, I think it's important that we all understand where we're headed. We can say things in this room that we cannot say in most circles.

"We know that our goal is one-world government. Environmentalism is simply a means to an end. We still don't know for certain if some of our environmental claims are valid. Questions remain about global warming. We're not even sure about carbon dioxide emissions and the ozone layer. But none of this matters.

"The overriding issue is to save the world from the scourge of war by banishing nationalism and religious strife from the face of the earth. Only world law and thus world government can accomplish this.

"So here's the plan. We must continually advocate world law through an ever-increasing number of international treaties. We must launch a relentless campaign for the establishment of an international court system. We cannot have enforceable world law without a world court. We also will need to promote the creation of a world tax. Without independent funding, the United Nations will always be at the mercy of the nations that hold the purse strings.

"It will be important to exploit every world development to argue in favor of these international structures. We must increasingly use international tribunals to deal with genocide, war crimes and crimes against humanity. This is particularly important when it comes to heads-of-state. The message needs to be sent loud and clear that no one is above international law. Once this principle is firmly established in our world, national leaders will be much more reluctant to do anything that might be a violation of international law. One or two high-profile trials of former heads-of-state, as the opportunity presents itself, will instill the proper respect for world law."

Morris spoke up. "One last thing. In everything that is said in promoting the future one-world government, it is important we always refer to it as global governance, not world government."

The Secretary General asked curiously, "Don't you think the average person will figure out that global governance and world government is the exact same thing?"

Michael shook his head. "No, they won't. You can't believe how simplistic people can be. They are sheep that want to be led. And we will lead them."

With that, the meeting was adjourned.

Chapter Fourteen

Michael and Rada boarded a plane for Hawaii the next morning. They wanted a few days of relaxation after their rigorous involvement in the Save the Earth Summit. It was always good to step back from the forest in order to be able to take another look at the trees. They also wanted to catch their breath before laying plans for the future.

After settling into their private chalet, they headed out to a secluded beach where they could relax, free of intrusions. Michael lay back in his lounge chair. It felt so good to empty his mind and do nothing. He knew the opportunity would be short-lived, but, for now, it was the tonic he needed. He looked at Rada and smiled. She was as beautiful as ever.

Rada reached over, taking his hand. They both knew what the other was thinking..."Yes," she agreed, "It would be nice to live like this all the time without the suffocating responsibilities of global leadership.

75

But neither of us could stand it. This will be good for a day or two, but then we will be chomping at the bit to get back to saving the world." Rada squeezed Michael's hand lightly and then let go–laying her head back to soak in the sun. Around 4 p.m., Michael and Rada returned to the beach house to shower and dress for dinner.

It was impossible for Michael to go anywhere in the world and not be recognized. Consequently, his secret service entourage had arranged a private room in a very exquisite restaurant situated right along the ocean. They escorted the Arachevs through a back door into the prepared room. It was serene and lovely.

Rada ordered the seafood platter, while Michael ordered lobster and steak. As they waited for their food to arrive, Michael's eyes swept over Rada appreciatively. For the first time, he noticed the ornament dangling at the hollow of her neck. He didn't remember seeing it before. Reaching over, he took the jewelry in his hand, examining it. It was a circle on a chain. Inside the chain was a pentagram.

"Where did you get this?" Michael inquired.

"Oh, Barbara gave that to me. Do you like it?"

"Well, it's nice. I'll admit that I was a little startled to see the pentagram," Michael said apprehensively.

"You know, Michael," Rada began, "I experienced a strange attraction to the pentagram the day we toured the Wiccan worship site on the Morris' ranch. When Barbara explained to me the meaning of the pentagram, I identified with it immediately." Holding the jewelry in her hand, she continued, "Do you remember what these five points of the pentagram stand for?"

"Remind me."

With barely concealed excitement, Rada held the pentagram so Michael could see. "The pentagram involves the earth and its environment. Each point stands for an element of nature. I think that's why it attracted me so much. This first point stands for fire, the second for air, the third for water, the fourth for earth, and the top point represents spirit." Hesitating, Rada then went on, "You know, Michael, I've been thinking that this could almost be the symbol of the environmental movement."

"Rada, don't ever say that to anyone else! I can hear the conservative talk-show hosts now—'ladies and gentlemen: the symbol for witchcraft has now become the official symbol of the environmental wackos'."

"I know. I know," Rada laughed. "For public relations reasons, it would never fly. But, to those of us who know there is no God or devil, we realize how appropriate it would be."

Taking the pentagram in his hand and looking at it one more time, Michael said with a smile, "I must admit, I do like it."

After dinner back at the beach house, Rada turned on the TV. CNN, NBC, Fox, all the major networks were discussing the Save the Earth Summit, Agenda 21, sustainable development, carbon dioxide emissions and global warming. Some of the commentators were pro-environmentalism. Some were against. Nevertheless, they were talking about it. Michael looked at Rada, grinning, "You know what they say, 'Kiss me or slap me. Just don't ignore me'."

When they awoke the next morning, the sun was glimmering across the Pacific Ocean. They had planned another day at the beach. However, Rada knew her husband too well. She immediately sensed in him that driving restlessness to get back to his mission.

"You're not wanting to go to the beach today, are you?" she asked with a knowing smile.

"Not really," Michael returned a little apologetically.

"It's okay," Rada assured. "I'm tired of doing nothing anyway."

"Maybe we can relax here in the room and brainstorm together," Michael suggested. "We don't have to feel pressured, but still we can work if we want to. Sometimes that's when we get our best work done."

"Sounds good to me," Rada agreed. "Let's do it!"

After the breakfast brought by the secret service, Michael sat in the lounge chair beside the window. Already, Rada could see the wheels turning in his mind. She pulled out the notebook that she always carried with her for occasions such as this.

Michael began talking. "We first need to redefine our goals." Rada wrote as Michael talked. "Of course, our all-encompassing long-range goal is the establishment of one-world government," Michael said matter-of-factly.

"Interim goals that will lead us to our ultimate destination include: strengthening the UN; establishing a World Court; creation of a global tax; unifying the world's religions. Am I forgetting anything?" Michael asked.

Rada spoke up, "There's one more thing that's important, but its pretty much taking care of itself. That's the global economy. Since the World Bank, the International Monetary Fund and the World Trade Organization are now so universal in their scope, a one-world economy is virtually assured."

"That's certainly an important element that must be continually monitored," Michael responded. "And without economic union, everything else begins to breakdown."

"Okay, I think that summarizes our critical goals," Rada said with considerable satisfaction. "Now for the fun. How do we get from here to there?"

"Rada, our plan will have to be altered many times between now and the ultimate realization of our goal," Michael responded. "But let's create a preliminary plan for the accomplishment of each of our short-term goals. This will keep us on track as we move toward our target."

"The first goal is to strengthen the UN," Rada prompted.

"And how can we do that?" Michael responded thoughtfully. "We must devise ways to transfer sovereignty from the national level of government to the world level. We should encourage multilateral action and discourage nations from acting alone. The Gulf War of 1991 is a great example of that. President Bush assembled a coalition of nations to act in solidarity against Saddam Hussein. Out of that grew the understanding that international conflicts should be solved by action from the world community. This kind of thinking must be continually fostered.

"The world's thinking needs to evolve until any unilateral military action taken without prior UN approval is considered a war crime. Eventually, the world community will make all decisions concerning war and peace.

"We must promote the teaching of Agenda 21 in all high schools and colleges around the world. We also must encourage the governments of the world, through persistent environmental conferences, to adopt the principles of Agenda 21 into law.

"We need to form a global environmental organization that can continually author new treaties to meet specific environmental needs. This environmental organization would then lobby the governments to ratify the treaties, bringing them into the status of law. These treaties would affect every aspect of governmental, business and private life.

"An annual Forum on World Affairs could be held to keep the dream of one-world government before the minds of the world's key influencers. This will be a very high-level meeting, and attendance will be by invitation only.

"The second goal must be the establishment of a World Court," Rada reminded.

Michael agreed, "We are already way down the road to accomplishing that one. Of course, a world court system has been envisioned since 1948. The International Tribunals of Rwanda, Yugoslavia and others are preparing the world to accept a permanent standing World Court. Our friends at the World Federalists Organization understand how central this is to the achievement of world government. I know they will be happy to lead the charge toward an international court system."

"And the global tax?" Rada questioned.

Michael grimaced, "You know how difficult that one is going to be. Nations never want to surrender financial control. The old adage, 'He who has the gold, makes the rules' is still true. At first, we will have to concentrate on some kind of tax on international activity—perhaps international air travel, international financial transactions or something similar. But Rada, we must find a way to get this done. To claim independence of action for our world government structures without financial independence is an illusion. One thing we can do is present the idea to the world over and over until people finally start getting used to it."

"Next, how do we go about unifying the world religiously?" Rada asked. This had become her area of interest over the years.

"As you know from touring the Samuels' ranch, this work is quite far advanced," Michael reminded her. "There is a meeting of the Parliament of the World's Religions that will be held next year in Chicago. Buddhists, Sikhs, Bahais, Zorastrians, Muslims, Christians and even Wiccans will be attending with the stated purpose of seeking common ground. I have friends at the UN who dream of establishing a United Religions Organization after the pattern of the United Nations. We will encourage it. That will be a huge step toward unity."

"Which brings us to our final area of discussion: global economy. As you said, everything is pretty much on track with the World Trade Organization."

"There is one more long-range need as far as the economy goes," Michael explained. "You don't fully control people until you control them economically. We will eventually need economic control over each individual in order to achieve true world government. However, we're not nearly ready for that stage yet."

By afternoon, Michael and Rada had hammered out their game plan. The outline looked something like this:

Blueprint for World Government

Long-term goal
   A world government including every nation and individual on the planet.

Short-term goals
   Strengthen the UN
   Establish a World Court
   Create a global tax
   Unify the world's religions
   Solidify the global economy

The Plan

Strengthen the UN
> Transfer sovereignty from nations to the UN
> Promote international law by every possible means
> Promote multilateralism; condemn unilateralism
> Promote Agenda 21
> Establish a global environmental organization
> Gain control over nations through environmental treaties
> Annual Forum on World Affairs

Establish a World Court
> Encourage efforts of the World Federalists Organization

Creation of a global tax
Continual promotion

Unify the world's religions
> Parliament of the World's Religions
> Birth of the United Religions Organization

Solidify the global economy
> Strengthen the World Trade Organization
> Devise a means of individual economic control

Chapter Fifteen

The next big meeting on the globalist agenda was the Parliament of the World's Religions.

A special planning session was held nine months prior to the conference. Cardinal Azinger, the head of the Secretariat for Interfaith Dialogue for the Roman Catholic Church, was there. The eminent Catholic theologian, Hans Zorich, attended. Imam Erekab representing the Muslim community, as well as Rabbi Rikin from Israel, and Buddhist Singh Ming, attended. These religious leaders were handpicked based on their allegiance to a future world government, and their vision of religious unity within that government. Then there were Michael and Rada Arachev and Morris and Barbara Samuels.

Morris was first to address the gathering.

"Ladies and gentlemen: It is with great pleasure that I speak to such a prestigious and esteemed group of leaders. All of you are infinitely aware of the danger in which our world presently finds itself. With enough nuclear firepower sitting on the launching pads of the world to destroy all human, plant and animal life one hundred times over, how could anyone be complacent?

"Since religious strife is the number one cause of war on earth, what we are gathered here to do takes on critical importance. The future existence of the world may well depend on the success of the upcoming Parliament of the World's Religions!

"If we fail in our efforts to bring about one-world government, one-world religion and a global economy, someday a conflict will be ignited that will burn the human house to the ground! Understanding this stark reality, the number one goal of the coming parliament must be to align the religious leaders of the world solidly behind the emerging one-world government. These leaders must leave Chicago with the clear-cut understanding that religious differences must be laid aside for the sake of the world community. What good will all our religions do if mankind is annihilated?"

Morris drove the point home with power and clarity. By the time he was finished, everyone in the room was nodding in agreement.

Imam Erekab rose to his feet. "Friends," he began, "if any one knows what radicalism is, we from the Muslim community do." It was obvious, by the expressions on all of the faces in the room, such candor was greatly appreciated. The Imam continued, "The time has come for each of us to admit we do not have an exclusive claim to the truth. We think we know who God is, but do we? Some call him Allah, some Jehovah, others Jesus, and we all think we are right! But we do not know for sure.

"The time has come for all of us to humble ourselves. This world-threatening religious strife must stop. I strongly suspect that, when we finally meet God, Allah will be the same as Jehovah, and Jehovah will be the same as Jesus. Religious exclusiveness is pride. Religious exclusiveness is sin. The time has come for mankind to turn a corner, discovering the common brotherhood of all of God's creation."

"Incredible!" Arachev thought to himself. "I never thought I would hear such words from the lips of a Muslim!" Everyone applauded as the Imam was seated.

The religious heavyweight at this meeting was the reputed Catholic theologian, Hans Zorich. He walked slowly to the front of the room. "Gentlemen, ladies," he began. "I'm so honored to be invited to this planning session for one of the most important meetings ever held on Mother Earth. Our cause is critical, and our motives are noble.

"Please allow me to remind you that beliefs still rule the world. We must present a document to the world from the upcoming parliament that expresses the principles, which will bind our planet together spiritually. Remember this: If people can't say it, they can't think it or believe it. Where would the Muslim movement be without the Koran? Where would Jews and Christians be without the Bible? Where would the United States be without the Constitution? This Interfaith movement will not become a movement unless we articulate the principles that express our reason for being.

"This document must express the lofty ideals of mankind. It must capture the core values that I am convinced all religions share. And it must lead us all to subjugate our own beliefs to this new global ethic for the greater common good of the human race."

Arachev was so moved by the brilliance and logic of the scholar, he immediately suggested that Zorich be entrusted with authoring the global ethic so that it could be presented to the parliament. Agreement was unanimous.

After the planning session had adjourned, the Arachevs were invited up to the Samuels' suite for a private dinner.

When they settled into the sitting room, Morris turned to Michael. "Well, what did you think?"

"I thought it went marvelously," Michael quickly replied. "Of course, we were preaching to the choir. We were all convinced before we arrived here. It's easy to persuade those already converted."

Arachev continued, "I've been a head-of-state. If we think we can govern the world through persuasion alone, we are kidding ourselves. Everything that we are presently doing will someday have to be written into law.

"Let me give you an example," Michael continued with considerable passion. "Imam Erekab expressed a profound truth when he said that religious exclusiveness is sin. The term 'religious exclusiveness' is the best expression of the enemy we fight. The Imam may well believe every word he spoke, but most of his followers do not. They will only be brought into conformity when the principles expressed by Imam Erekab are enacted into enforceable law."

"Wait a minute, Michael," Barbara broke in. "How do you ever expect to do such a thing? Do you anticipate regulating the form of a person's religion by law? I doubt that would ever work."

"No, no, no," Arachev replied quickly. "They can keep whatever religion they want. It's *speaking* against any other religion that we will have to control. That's when conflict occurs. You know what history has taught us. During the Inquisition, it was 'be baptized or die.' During the Crusades, their slogan was 'By this sign, conquer.' Even today, Christians believe they are commissioned to 'Preach the gospel to every creature.' And that stirs up religious hatred. It's when I think my religion is better than yours, or you think yours is better than mine that the seeds of war are planted.

"That's the reason I was so struck by the Imam's term 'religious exclusiveness.' We must outlaw religious exclusiveness!" Michael declared vehemently.

The time for the Parliament of the World's Religions rolled around quickly. The spacious Palmer House Hilton had never witnessed such a spectacle of veils, turbans, yarmulkes, cowls, and cassocks. Ministers and monks mingled with rabbis and Rastafarians. Egyptian priests and priestesses in exotic headdresses glided silently by African elders wearing beautiful prints of intense colors.

Over 6,500 delegates, representing approximately 125 of the world's religions participated in the Parliament. Muslims, Buddhists, Jews, Protestants, Roman Catholics, Hindus, Jains, Zoroastrians, among others, were gathered in hopes of reaching agreement on a universal declaration of human values. They also harbored dreams of laying the groundwork for a future organization akin to a United Nations of Religions.

The Parliament's schedule was designed so that the various religious leaders would have a chance to witness and, if desired, participate in the worship rituals of the other religions.

The beating of drums could be heard down one hall as the Africans danced and whirled feverishly during their worship. The Muslims stood praying toward Mecca. They followed the same ritual Michael had witnessed before his meeting with Imam Khaled al-Hassan. Next door, Jews stood beneath their prayer shawls with their phylacteries wound around their hands. They bobbed back and forth as they prayed from their prayer books. The forms of worship were as varied as the religions represented at the summit.

Barbara and Rada enjoyed observing the diverse forms of worship. They were unusual and varied, and yet at times quite similar. One afternoon, after exploring several religious groups, they came upon the area designated for the Wiccans. The witches' evening ritual was just beginning. Rada again found herself strangely drawn to the symbolism of the Wiccans. Everything they did seemed to acknowledge the connection between the human race and the earth.

Rada could understand this religion. The earth gives food, warmth, water, and life. From dust thou art, to dust thou shalt return. Rada looked at the circle. She thought to herself, "Life is one big circle between earth and humankind." As she stood in contemplation, her fingers inadvertently tightened around the pentagram at her neck. She looked at the symbols: fire, water, air, earth, spirit. Once again, she felt the strange pull of the Wiccan's worship as it took place under the stars.

Arachev was not scheduled to speak during the Parliament. Yet he met with the key religious leaders many times during the next nine days. It was obvious to Michael that exposing people to different religions created an appreciation for different forms of worship. There was a warmth caused by the tolerance and respect shared among the different religious attendees.

Throughout the Parliament, key leaders had been carefully going over the global ethic prepared by theologian, Hans Zorich. He had done a superb job. Only minor changes were suggested to his original work.

Now came the time for selling this new common spirituality. It was critical that the delegates buy into the new ethic. They, in turn, would be counted on to sell it to all of their followers.

It was the last afternoon when Hans Zorich stepped to the rostrum of the large convention hall where all 6,500 delegates had gathered. He stood for a moment drinking in the diverse religious crowd with his eyes. Suddenly, raising both arms high, he swung them outward in an all-encompassing gesture. "My brothers and my sisters," he called in a loud voice. "A new day for the world has dawned this week in the city of Chicago. Together we have made a decision to put religious conflict to rest forever. As religious leaders, we are leading our world into a new day of unity and oneness.

"I embrace you, my brothers and my sisters, I embrace you, Protestants. I embrace you, Jews and Muslims. My arms enfold you, Buddhists and Zoroastrians. We are not as divided as the forces of disunity would lead us to believe." Suddenly, applause began to break out across the convention hall. The staccato clapping of hands seemed to cause the crowd to spring to life. Soon there was rhythmic foot stomping, which then turned into dancing and rejoicing. Together, Catholic, Jew, Buddhist and Muslims celebrated the dawning of a new day–a day when the world's religions would come together in unity for the common good of all humankind.

The spontaneous celebration continued for 20 minutes. Hans Zorich stood at the podium beaming. Finally, he motioned with his hands for attention. The crowd returned to their seats ready to listen.

"My dear brothers and sisters, we know what we have felt this afternoon, and we will never forget it. But there are six billion people who are not here today. They didn't experience the oneness and brotherhood we have experienced. It now becomes our responsibility and privilege to convey it to them.

"How do you transmit something like this? Is it possible? I say 'yes.' We must take words home with us–an expression of the common ground that we have discovered at the Parliament of the World's Religions."

Pulling the prepared Global Ethic from his pocket, he continued. "Each of you will leave here with a copy of this Global Ethic. It embodies the spirit of this Parliament. You must absorb it into your heart. Then you must sow it into the hearts of others.

"Let me read a sample of the powerful unifying truths that will now begin to change the human race:

"We are women and men who have embraced the precepts and practices of the world's religions:

"Already, ancient guidelines for human behavior exist which are found in the teachings of the religions of the world, and which are the conditions for a sustainable world order.

"Opening our hearts to one another, we must set aside our minor differences for the cause of world community." I don't think any of the preceding two paragraphs should be changed since these are actual quotes from the Parliament of the World's Religions, which was actually held."

Lifting his voice, Zorich continued, "Ladies and gentlemen, these brief excerpts reflect the heart and spirit of the new Global Ethic for human behavior. I hereby propose the adoption of the Global Ethic by acclamation. If you will join me, please stand."

All 6,500 delegates rose to their feet as one. The applause built until it reached a thunderous crescendo. Soon the dancing and celebration took on a life of its own. The Interfaith movement was born!

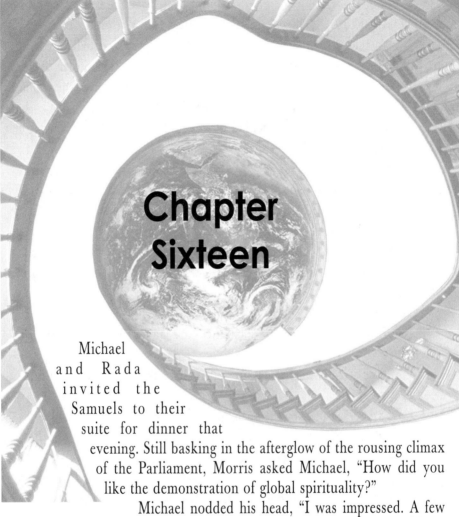

Chapter Sixteen

Michael and Rada invited the Samuels to their suite for dinner that evening. Still basking in the afterglow of the rousing climax of the Parliament, Morris asked Michael, "How did you like the demonstration of global spirituality?"

Michael nodded his head, "I was impressed. A few years ago, I would never have believed that we would be this far down the road to religious unity. I was afraid the problem of religious conflict might derail our efforts toward our New World Order. What we witnessed over the past nine days was more than a few extreme religious liberals. We saw 6,500 delegates that are ready to lay aside religious differences for the sake of the world community. I truly believe this is a movement that will sweep away any outdated religious thinking that tries to get in its way."

After dinner, Michael asked Morris, "Where do you think we should go from here?"

"I think the time has come to launch the drive to establish a permanent world court," Morris stated emphatically. "Without a court system to give teeth to international law, global governance will never be anything but a feel-good theory. It may take some time for an idea of this magnitude to win acceptance. But if we don't get started now, the global court won't be ready by the time we need it."

"Where do we start?" Michael inquired. "Who can help us bring a world court to fruition?"

Morris snapped his fingers. "I've got it!" he exclaimed. "I know the exact person we need, and he's here at this meeting. Bill Baker of the World Federalist Movement is our man."

"Let's call him right now," Michael said excitedly. "Maybe he could come talk to us this evening."

Dialing the hotel operator, Morris requested Baker's room. "Hello. Bill Baker here."

"Hello, Bill. Morris Samuels."

"Morris! I haven't seen you since the Save the Earth Summit. Where are you?"

"Believe it or not, I'm right here in the Palmer House Hilton," Morris replied.

"You've been attending the Parliament?" Bill asked in surprise. "I never saw you. Of course, it's easy to miss someone in a crowd of over six thousand people. Is there a chance I'll get to see you before you leave?"

"Actually, that's the reason I'm calling," Morris explained. "I'm sitting here talking to my good friend, Michael Arachev. We've been discussing the need for a world court. Bill, you know more about that than anyone else I know. Would you have time to stop by my room for a few minutes?"

"Sure, my friend. I'd be glad to," Bill responded enthusiastically. "I'll be down in about thirty minutes."

While waiting for Baker, Morris filled Michael, Rada and Barbara in on the World Federalist Movement.

"The World Federalist Movement is a global citizens' movement with members and associated organizations around the globe. The WFM international secretariat is based in New York City, across from the United Nations. It was founded in 1947 in Montreux, Switzerland,

and brings together organizations and individuals committed to the vision of a just world order through a strengthened United Nations."

Rada raised her eyebrows. "So these people are serious about creating a New World Order!" she said.

"You'd better believe it," Morris responded. "They eat, drink, sleep and breathe their dream of a true one-world government."

When Bill Baker entered the room, Arachev was immediately impressed. Tall, with sandy-colored hair, Baker had a relaxed demeanor that made people want to work with him. Yet Arachev sensed an inner toughness that would persist until he got what he wanted.

Morris made the introductions. "Bill–Michael and Rada Arachev, and, of course, my wife Barbara." Turning to the three of them, he said, "Please meet my long-time friend, Bill Baker. Bill and I have worked together many times at the United Nations."

Settling into the large, overstuffed chair in the corner, Bill turned to Morris. "Okay, what's going on? You don't get a guy out of his pajamas at nine o'clock at night for nothing," he said with a smile.

In his usual blunt style, Michael laid their proposal on the table. "We want to see the formation of a permanent world court. Morris tells me that you're the one person who can get the job done."

"Oh, is that all?" Bill exclaimed. "I can see I won't be getting much sleep tonight."

Morris spoke up, "Bill, we know this is a formidable undertaking. But you know as well as I do that the system of international law, which has been painstakingly built over the last fifty years, is worthless without the mechanism to enforce it."

Arachev interceded, "We are ready to put all of our influence and our considerable resources behind your efforts if you will lead the way."

"So what's the game-plan?" Morris asked Bill, sensing Baker's willingness to assume the lead role in the project. He had no doubt that Bill would accept the challenge since he knew that his friend had dreamed of some day having a functioning court system at the global level.

Bill leaned forward in his chair as he began to speak, "Our biggest obstacle is overcoming the knee-jerk reaction that exists against world government. McCarthyism and the John Birch Society have done a job on the psyche of the average person. Fortunately, there is a new generation coming up that knows little of those irrational prejudices of the '50's and '60's."

"What do you propose?" Arachev anxiously broke in.

"We have some very powerful arguments in favor of establishing an international court system. Remember, it was a temporary international tribunal that brought Nazi war criminals to justice after World War II. But since that time, we have not had a court mechanism to try international criminals. Since nations have not been willing to prosecute their own former heads-of-state, most of the time these criminals have gotten off scot-free. For instance, Idi Amin is living somewhere in Saudi Arabia right now in a comfortable villa enjoying a carefree life of retirement. However, in more recent times, humanity has become repulsed by criminal governments not being held accountable for their crimes. I think the world is ready to begin dealing with some of these legalized international criminals," Bill concluded.

"Would Saddam Hussein qualify?" Barbara queried.

"Without a doubt," Baker replied. "Our challenge is to transition the world's thinking into accepting the concept of international justice. We have to be able to extradite even a head-of-state from his own nation, and force him to stand trial before an international tribunal. We have to decide how to best accomplish this."

"I know what to do," Arachev stated flatly. "We can establish temporary tribunals for specific situations when atrocities are committed. The anti-world-government crowd won't protest so loudly against what is officially a temporary situation. Once we bring a few particularly despicable international criminals to justice, global acceptance of a permanent international court will become possible."

Michael continued, "We already have several conflicts in the world that could lend themselves to charges of crimes against humanity and genocide. The ethnic clashes in Bosnia and Yugoslavia have already produced brutal actions by their rulers. Some of the tribal wars in Africa are resulting in the slaughter of thousands. I'm sure that, over the next few years, the need for international justice will become apparent.

"And you can count on some abuse of power occurring that will provide the perfect opportunity to implement temporary tribunals. It will happen," Arachev stated confidently.

"When the time comes, we will turn these international trials into show-trials. By then, the world will forget it was ever opposed to international tribunals. Then we can proceed to establish a permanent world court system.

"First, we have to begin the education process," Michael explained. "We need to encourage the press to publish articles that explain the need for international justice. Bill can speak on the subject at our next World Affairs Forum. The key people who influence world leaders will be there."

When Michael and Rada said good night to Bill Baker and the Samuels, they understood that another huge and very important step toward their goal of world government had just been taken.

Chapter Seventeen

For the next few years, Arachev remained largely out of the public view. He preferred it that way. If his activities were exposed to public scrutiny, he would have to scratch and claw for every inch gained. Away from the glare of the media spotlight, he was able to move forward with relative impunity. While the world was absorbed with Bill Clinton and Monica Lewinsky, he was assembling the structures of world government as fast as he could go. And Rada was always right by his side, making sure that they stuck to the plan they had created after the Save the Earth Summit.

Arachev met every six months with the national leaders of the Green Earth chapters that he had established around the world. The world's finest environmentalists were brought in to speak. The goal was to mobilize each chapter for the continual promotion of environmental treaties and laws. This kept the pressure on each national legislature to ratify the treaties that were increasingly strengthening international law. All of this was being done in the name of saving the earth. It was very difficult for nations to fight against such a cause.

The stronger international law became, the more it encroached upon national sovereignty. When a nation ratified an international treaty, it was required to change any national laws that contradicted the requirements of the treaty. Thus, national laws were increasingly forced to adopt the form of international law. This was not only true of environmental treaties, but with economic treaties and all other treaties that regulated relations between nations.

The Samuels and the Arachevs understood that the dream of world government didn't stand a chance unless the religions of the world could be brought together in harmony. When one of the speakers at the Parliament of the World's Religions had mentioned the need for a United Nations of Religions, a light had come on in Morris Samuel's brain. He had been turning the idea over and over in his mind since that time. How could it be done?

Suddenly he knew! The fiftieth birthday of the United Nations was just around the corner. What better commemoration than to hold a high-profile ecumenical service bringing political leaders and spiritual leaders from around the world together in celebration.

The next time Morris was with Michael Arachev, he shared his idea with him. "It's an excellent idea!" Michael immediately responded.

"I have a good friend by the name of Robert Mahli at the United Nations," Morris said. "He is the Under-Secretary General. Robert is a very spiritual person and has an appreciation for all faith traditions. I'm sure he would favor this idea."

"Let's call him now!"

Just as they expected, Mahli was immediately enthralled with the idea. Michael could hear his exclamation as Morris talked to him on the phone. "Morris, that is a marvelous idea. I'll see to it immediately."

As soon as Mahli hung up from talking with Morris, he began thinking about the way to proceed. Of course, the celebration would have to be held in San Francisco since that was where the United Nations Charter was adopted in 1945. "We need to have the ecumenical celebration on the exact date of the adoption of the charter–June 26th."

"Who could properly preside over this celebration and ensure that we achieve the desired result?" Mahli asked himself. It would have to be someone enthusiastic about Interfaithism.

All of a sudden, it dawned on him who the perfect person would be. He had met Bishop James Hanscom of the Episcopalian diocese in San Francisco at the Parliament of the World's Religions. A class act, Hanscom would be the perfect person to preside over the UN's fiftieth birthday celebration. One phone call and 15 minutes later, the wheels were set in motion.

On June 26, 1995, dignitaries from around the world filed into San Francisco's Grace Cathedral. Many heads-of-state were there along with foreign ministers, UN ambassadors and the usual globalist crowd. They had all come to commemorate the event that had ushered in a new era of humanity—the era of global government.

As Bishop Hanscom watched the various world leaders enter, he couldn't help but notice the camaraderie that existed between officials from the various countries. At the same time, it was obvious that the same relationship did not exist among the religious leaders that were present.

"Why is that?" Hanscom questioned himself. "What's the difference?" The answer was obvious. The difference was the United Nations. These political leaders met every day at the UN as they worked together to ensure a peaceful world. But the religious leaders never spoke to each other. "No wonder there is such a lack of inter-religious understanding," Hanscom thought to himself. "Why couldn't we form a United Nations of Religions?" he wondered.

Immediately after the commemorative service, Michael Arachev sought out Bishop Hanscom to congratulate him on a job well done. After the exchange of pleasantries, the Bishop asked, "Do you have a moment?"

"Certainly," Arachev nodded. "How may I assist you?"

Bishop Hanscom explained, "I noticed as the different people entered the meeting today that the political leaders of our world were very much at ease with one another. But there was considerable tension among the spiritual leaders."

Arachev nodded in agreement. "It's not a healthy situation," Michael replied. "What do you propose?"

"I believe the relationship the political leaders enjoy stems from the fact that they deal with one another on a daily basis at the UN. On the other hand, the religious leaders seldom even speak to each other. Michael, I want to form a United Nations of Religions."

"I think it's a wonderful idea," Arachev said immediately. "How can I help?"

Hanscom explained, "The first thing I want to do is to take a one-year goodwill tour. I want to personally visit the religious leaders of the world in order to share this vision with them, rallying their support."

"I think that is exactly what you should do," Arachev affirmed.

"Do you know of a source of funding for such a venture?" Hanscom inquired anxiously.

Michael paused for a moment, thinking. "I'm quite sure that the Lillian Endowment would be willing to supply whatever you need. Let's settle it right now," he said, reaching for his cell phone.

Arachev quickly explained to Marilyn Williams, his contact at Lillian, what the need was and how important this could be. "I'm sure we have funds available for such a worthy project," she replied.

After hanging up, Arachev looked at Hanscom smiling. "You're all set, my friend. Pack your bags. And tell the Pope that Michael Arachev said hello."

Later that evening, Michael recounted the events of the day to Rada. "Everything went off without a hitch, exactly as we planned. Sometimes I think the advance into world government is happening too easily. It almost seems too good to be true," Michael said with a touch of concern.

"Relax Michael," Rada smiled. "Remember, you are a man of destiny."

Chapter Eighteen

Through-
out the nineties
while most of the
world remained bliss-
fully unaware, events
moved swiftly toward world government.

The International Tribunal for Yugoslavia was established by the UN to prosecute acts of genocide and crimes against humanity. Shortly thereafter, an International Tribunal for Rwanda was set up. Proceedings at these tribunals ensured that the power of international justice would be continually showcased before the world community. Both of these tribunals were temporary courts established to deal with one particular conflict. While reporting on the ongoing trials, it was not uncommon for journalists to include the observation that a permanent international court was needed instead of these ad hoc tribunals cobbled together to deal with a particular emergency.

Bishop Hanscom returned home from his world religious tour to considerable fanfare from the media. He had visited the Archbishop of Canterbury, Bishop Desmond Tutu, the Dalai Lama, the Pope and Mother Teresa, along with many others. He reported that religious leaders everywhere felt that his proposal for a United Nations of Religions was an idea whose time had come.

Hanscom announced that a charter-writing conference for the envisioned United Religions would be held in 1996. Each year thereafter, a charter-writing conference would be held during the week of June 26, the date of the signing of the UN Charter. It was decided that the actual charter signing and the birth of the United Religions would take place on June 26, 2000, exactly 55 years after the signing of the UN Charter.

The year 1997 proved particularly pivotal for the global planners. As usual, they held their secret annual strategy session in January during the first weekend of the New Year. The meeting was held at the Samuels' ranch in Colorado. Each participant arrived separately and discreetly in order to not attract unwanted media coverage.

After breakfast on Saturday morning, everyone gathered into the spacious conference room that the Samuels had built for such occasions. A hot fire was blazing in the eight-foot fireplace at the end of the room. The Arachevs and Samuels were there. The maverick media mogul Theodore Joiner, Bill Baker of the World Federalist Movement, and Robert Mahli from the UN were among the participants. Bishop James Hanscom was attending the meeting for the first time. He had been invited as the special guest of Michael Arachev. Alan Black from the World Bank was present representing the economic sphere. Simon Peters, who ran the day-to-day operations of Green Earth International, was sitting to the right of Michael Arachev. The Secretary General of the United Nations, and the President of the United States were there, as well.

Barbara Samuels gave the welcome, "Hello, everyone. Morris and I welcome you to our private getaway. I hope your rooms are comfortable. We do apologize for the frigid temperatures outside, but I hope you're enjoying the delicious warmth of our fireplace. Doesn't it feel good?" Everyone in the room applauded.

Barbara continued, "If you need anything at all during your stay, please let me know. I will make sure that you have it. Thanks for coming."

Morris Samuels stood with his back to the fireplace. "Please let me add my welcome to Barbara's. What a pleasure to see all of you again!

"We always begin this meeting by going over our scorecard. During the past year, the awareness of international law has jumped significantly. The Tribunals of Rwanda and Yugoslavia have contributed tremendously to this positive development. The continued adoption of international treaties has also been a major factor. To date, 214 international treaties have been registered with the United Nations. Each of these treaties contains hundreds of pages of regulations. They cover such things as: War Crimes and Crimes against Humanity, Trade Practices, Discrimination against Women, International Postal Regulations, Convention against Torture, Rights of the Child, Emission of Carbon Dioxide, Taxation of Road Vehicles, Issuance and Validity of Driving Permits, and the International Coffee Agreement. I only cite these few examples so that you can appreciate the far reach of international law. These treaties cover virtually every area of human behavior."

Samuels continued, "It's so nice to have Bishop Hanscom with us. A huge step into the future was taken during this past year. Under Bishop Hanscom's dynamic leadership, the first charter-writing session was held to create a United Nations of Religion. Since religion has been the chief cause of war on earth, the movement toward a United Religions Organization is significant progress.

"A major development toward the governance of nations is this year's passage of the Comprehensive Nuclear-Test-Ban Treaty. One of our prime goals is to completely rid the world of nuclear weapons. We will never be able to fully implement global governance until all nuclear weapons have been abolished. How can the United Nations possibly discipline a nation if that nation can threaten major population centers with total destruction?

"There have been many other important developments in our drive toward global government, but from my perspective, those I have mentioned are the highpoints for the past year. Although we have accomplished a great deal, there is still much work to do."

Next came everyone's favorite time—brainstorming. This was when everybody present offered ideas for the promotion of world government. It didn't matter how unorthodox the suggestions were.

As usual, Theodore Joiner went first. "I'll tell you," he said. "I've been watching some things. It's not political conflict that blocks world unity. Why, we have communists and capitalists barbecuing together. We have Chinese and Americans playing Ping-Pong. The Berlin Wall is down, and Germany is reunited. I'm not sure that high-schoolers even know the difference between communism and capitalism anymore. As a matter of fact, I'm not sure there is a difference. They have simply intermingled.

"As I see it, the big problem is the fighting among the religions. We have Muslims screaming that there's no other God but Allah and Mohammed is his prophet. The Christians contend that Jesus is the only way to salvation. Now, we think this problem will somehow take care of itself. But it never does. These passions will continue to build until, ultimately, there will be a war. I think we need to bring the top one thousand religious leaders in the world to the UN. We must explain to them that they can either sabotage peace on earth or they can facilitate it.

"These religious leaders control what people believe and feel. They speak to their followers on a weekly basis. Many times, they control the schools that educate the younger generation. I have concluded that we will never build a new world order of peace and security without marrying politics to religion."

As Joiner spoke, the force of his logic carried every person in the room with him. Heads nodded in agreement.

"You know, we've never brought religion into the UN," the UN Secretary General spoke up abruptly.

"And that's the very reason the UN finds itself at a dead-end right now," Joiner replied quickly. "We've advanced world unity as far as possible without the religious element. We have no choice."

"You still haven't answered how you expect to accomplish this," the Secretary General challenged.

Joiner leaned back in his chair locking his hands behind his head. With a big smile, he said, "Why don't you trust me with this one. I have a little plan in the back of my brain that I think will work. Let's just say that this will be my personal project."

It was obvious that Joiner had said all he was going to say. But everyone in the room knew they had not heard the last of his plan. Once the media mogul got a bee in his bonnet, he didn't rest until he saw the matter through.

"There's something else that I think has become urgent. And I think the time for us to act is now." All eyes turned to Bill Baker from the World Federalist Movement. Bill continued, "Moral leadership and leading by persuasion only works for so long. Our web of international law will remain as weak as water unless we give birth to the necessary enforcement mechanisms."

"Of course, you're speaking of a world court with independent power to prosecute violators of international law," Arachev interjected.

"Yes," Baker agreed.

"And you believe the world is ready to accept a world court?" Morris Samuels asked inquisitively.

Baker replied quickly, "All of you know I have advocated a world court system for the last twenty years. I keep my fingers on the pulse of public opinion. The demands we are receiving at the World Federalist Movement for a world court system are getting louder and louder. I'm telling you, the time has come to get this done."

"You know Bill, I agree with you," Arachev said, leaning forward. He knew how important this was. They could not afford to fail. "The window of opportunity might not open again for a very long time. The one nation on earth that could sabotage the effort for a world court is the United States." Turning to the President, he said, "Mr. President, you can guarantee the success of this endeavor."

The President responded, "What do you have in mind, Michael?"

Arachev explained, "When you make your welcome speech to this year's UN General Assembly, I think you need to present the proposal for the creation of the International Criminal Court. It must come from you."

All eyes were on the President. He sat quietly, turning the pros and cons over in his mind. Everyone in the room knew that he was an internationalist to the core of his being. But he was being asked to take a considerable political risk. Finally, looking around at each of the powerful people in the room, he said, "I'll do it."

"Great!" Joiner thrust his fist out in front of him in jubilation. "We've been needing to get this done for a long time." He was definitely the least inhibited person in the room. Everyone in the room applauded.

Michael thought to himself, "This will be a crucial step on the road to the New World Order!"

Barbara Samuels spoke next. "Bishop Hanscom, how is the charter for the United Religions coming along?" she asked. "Are your efforts meeting with success?"

"Yes," Hanscom answered with a broad smile. "We have already written much of the charter. The meetings are mainly to provide validation of the document from the different religions. We intend to be on schedule for the birth of the United Religions. Of course, each meeting gives us a chance for world-wide press coverage, which helps us to build global support."

Simon Peters from Green Earth International spoke next. "Most of you know by now that this year we are hoping for the adoption of the most far-reaching environmental controls in the history of the world. The Kyoto Environmental Conference will be held in Kyoto, Japan in December.

"We have already drawn up definite plans for sustainable development. We are planning a full court press to get every major nation to sign the Kyoto Protocol. Kyoto will set standards for hydrocarbon emissions that must be met by certain dates. If the major industrialized nations do not meet their goals, heavy fines will be levied against them. This money will then be used to help developing countries."

Arachev broke in. "Are these goals achievable?" he asked.

"Theoretically, yes," Peters replied. "In reality, no. But meeting quotas is not the main concern," he explained. "We have a solution that will help the underdeveloped countries and, at the same time, will accelerate the equal distribution of the world's wealth.

"Here's how it will work," Peters continued. "When one of the wealthy nations exceeds its quota of emissions, it can purchase part of the quota of an undeveloped country that doesn't use all of its allotment. The price to purchase emission credits will be quite high, but this will allow the nation in violation to avoid heavy fines by the international community. At the same time, it provides developing nations with the money that they need to raise living standards to the world level."

"I love it!" Morris Samuels exclaimed. "It is simply ingenious! In one stroke, we bring every nation under the power of international law; we promote clean air and fight global warming; and we redistribute the world's wealth so that all nations become equal."

When the meeting was concluded, everyone understood that they had their marching orders for the rest of the year. The goals they had set were big—even huge. But the bigger the goal, the higher the motivation. The group disbanded with great anticipation for what the year would hold.

As the participants left the Samuels' ranch, one question loomed in their minds—"What did Theodore Joiner have up his sleeve?"

Chapter Nineteen

After everyone had left, the Arachevs and the Samuels relaxed by the fire.

"Well, what do you think?" Michael asked, turning to Morris and Barbara. "Did we accomplish our goals?"

"I'm excited," Barbara exclaimed. "I feel like we're on the brink of real progress. Once the world court is in place, we will truly have a functioning world government."

Morris spoke up. "You know me," he said. "As a dyed-in-the-wool environmentalist, I'm excited at the prospect of the Kyoto Treaty. I think it is especially ingenious that the wealthy nations will have to buy allotments of clean air from the have-not nations. This will allow us to redistribute the world's wealth without people ever realizing what we're doing."

Rada always knew when Michael had something on his mind. She decided to create the opening for him. "Michael, were you happy with the meeting?"

"Why sure. Absolutely," Michael replied quickly. Then he hesitated.

Morris prodded, "Something's bothering you. Tell us what it is."

Michael began to speak slowly, thoughtfully. "During the entire session, I kept feeling that something fundamental was missing. It was as though we weren't hitting the jugular. Do any of you know what I mean?" he asked, his gaze moving from one to the other.

He continued, "I still think there's one thing we must have. We need a unifying creed. All great movements have a creed—a holy book. The Muslims have the Koran. Jews have the Torah, Christians have the Bible, and Communists have the *Communist Manifesto*. I don't think we'll ever achieve the world unity we are after without a statement of beliefs that can be taught at every level of life. Only when the people of the world believe the same will they truly be united."

"I see what you're driving at now," Morris responded. "And I think I agree with you. But where would we start?"

"Maybe we could use Agenda 21," Barbara suggested.

"Have you ever tried to read that thing?" Morris asked. "As much as I believe in it, it's like trying to eat sawdust!" They all nearly fell over in the floor in peals of laughter.

"That's obviously not the answer," Barbara admitted, still laughing. "So, what is the answer?"

"I think we have to create it," Rada stated flatly. "We have to write it. Nothing else will work."

Morris nodded. "Actually, Michael, you have to write it. Let's not kid ourselves. You've been the prime force behind the drive for world government ever since your days as President of the Soviet Union.

"Obviously, you already have a vision for this or you wouldn't have brought it up. This is a job that simply cannot be done by a committee. I think you have to give birth to it." The others in the room nodded in agreement.

"You're probably right," Michael conceded. "It won't be easy, but I'll do it."

Many years before, Michael had understood the power of the environment to remove barriers between people and nations. When threatened with the prospect of extinction, even bitter enemies became willing to cooperate together. He had no doubt in his mind that the Global Creed should have a strong environmental emphasis. At the same time, he felt that it must somehow contain a spiritual dimension.

He wrestled with the problem. How do you bring environmentalism and spirituality together? All of a sudden, it dawned on him! He had read it in the Temple of Understanding at Morris and Barbara's ranch: "The environment is a religious issue."

That was his task. He had to convince the people of the world that the earth was sacred. Those who would damage Mother Earth destroyed the very thing that sustained their own lives. Once this came together in his mind, he realized it might not be that difficult. After all, the earth gives us our food, water–the very essentials of life. Without it, we would all die. So the earth is actually the source of our life. "They who sin against Mother Earth, sin against their own souls," Michael thought.

Michael was awake deep into the night working on the Global Creed. He was attempting to assimilate the concepts that all human beings must agree on in order to build a sustainable and peaceful world order. As major themes surfaced in his mind, he wrote them down. By dawn, he had an outline. It looked like this:

Global Creed

Preamble

Humankind must join together to create a sustainable global society. The foundations of this global society must be: respect for nature, universal human rights, economic justice, and a culture of peace.

The protection and care of Mother Earth is a sacred trust.

Recent patterns of production and consumption must be curtailed. They are no longer sustainable.

The gap between rich and poor is widening. This must be rectified by fair distribution of wealth.

The increase of human population has overburdened the earth's infrastructure. Population must be controlled.

Our choice: Form a global partnership to care for the Earth and each other, or risk destruction of ourselves and of life, as we know it.

The world must now undergo a radical value shift. We must learn to live simply that others may simply live.

We must cultivate a sense of global citizenship. All humankind is now interdependent.

We urgently need a shared vision of basic values to provide an ethical foundation for the emerging world community.

Therefore, we affirm the following interdependent principles for a sustainable way of life as a common standard by which the conduct of all individuals, organizations, businesses, governments, and transnational institutions is to be guided and assessed.

Principles
Every human being is responsible to promote the common good.

We must adopt, at all levels, sustainable development plans and regulations that make environmental conservation and rehabilitation integral to all development initiatives.

Patterns of production, consumption, and reproduction should be adopted that safeguard Earth's regenerative capacities, human rights, and community well-being.

The eradication of poverty must be accomplished by promoting the equitable distribution of wealth within nations and among nations.

It is imperative that we integrate into formal education and life-long learning the knowledge, values, and skills needed for a sustainable way of life.

Now—A new beginning
The road of promise that we envision requires a change of mind and heart. It requires a new sense of global interdependence and universal responsibility.

Sometimes important values conflict. We must find ways to harmonize diversity with unity, the exercise of freedom with the common good.

In order to build a sustainable global community, the nations of the world must renew their commitment to the United Nations, and do everything possible to strengthen it.

Finally—the principles of this Global Creed must be incorporated into an international treaty that will be legally binding on all peoples of the earth.

When Michael was finished, he went over his work with great satisfaction. The case had been powerfully made for regulating every human activity on earth.

Michael smiled, thinking to himself, "The only way to fulfill this vision is to implement a totally planned global government. Talk about taking the world into socialism through the back door!" It was working exactly as he had planned years ago. "This is simply brilliant!" he exulted silently.

The resulting world socialist government was the one aspect of his plan that he couldn't share with anyone...except Rada, of course.

Chapter Twenty

The President made his promised speech at the opening of the UN General Assembly. His call for the establishment of an international criminal court went virtually unnoticed by the general public. But the globalists understood that the most powerful leader on earth was giving the green light for their long-desired world court. They immediately swung into action, wanting to strike while the iron was hot.

The World Federalist Association and Bill Baker had been preparing for this moment since the secret planning session in January. They sent the word out that a preparatory commission would start to work immediately on the structure of the new world court. Several preliminary planning sessions would take place before the actual court formation conference, which would be held in Rome beginning June 15, 1998.

By the time the Conference for the International Criminal Court was convened, most of the court's structure was set. The majority of the conference was devoted to how much independence the ICC prosecutor would have, and the definitions of the crimes over which the court would have jurisdiction.

The United States wanted all cases that were to appear before the court to be referred by the UN Security Council. This would give the U.S. control over which cases could be tried, since it possessed veto power on the Council. However, the nations of the world understood this, and did not want the U.S. to control the new court as it did most of the UN. They opted for an independent prosecutor with wide powers of jurisdiction.

Four categories of crimes were placed under the jurisdiction of the ICC: Crimes against Humanity, Genocide, War Crimes and Crimes of Aggression.

Arachev and Samuels stayed in constant contact with Bill Baker during both the preliminary conferences and the conference in Rome. They understood that this was a defining moment, and that the formation of a world court independent of the veto was the greatest leap forward in global governance since the formation of the United Nations itself in 1945.

To the average layperson, the categories of crimes seemed reasonable enough and rather innocuous. However, Arachev and company understood the implications of the powers being bestowed upon the new ICC.

Genocide was defined as causing physical harm or "mental harm" to a minority, whether it was a racial, sexual, or religious minority. Most of the delegates at the founding conference had no idea that causing mental harm was intended to control what people would be allowed to say or write. Hate crimes and hate speech would fall under this heading. The insiders understood that eventually religious exclusiveness and religious proselytizing would also fall under the heading of genocide. Arachev understood all of this very clearly since he had grown up under these types of laws in the Soviet Union.

During the conference, Syria and Egypt co-sponsored an amendment to the war crimes heading. This amendment added population transfer into occupied territories as a war crime. It was aimed directly at the nation of Israel, and everyone at the conference knew it. It was passed anyway.

The most telling of all the elements was the Crime of Aggression. The intent was to outlaw any military action by any country without prior UN approval. Though most of the delegates at the conference were dyed-in-the-wool globalists, even they knew the nations of the world were not yet ready for this total surrender of national sovereignty.

The disagreement over this issue was so sharp that it threatened the entire effort. Finally, a compromise was struck. Defining Crimes of Aggression would be postponed. That category of crime would not be prosecutable until agreement could be reached on the definition.

On July 17th, the vote to accept the International Criminal Court Statute of Rome was taken. It was approved 120 to 7. The final draft was such an infringement on national sovereignty that the United States, whose president proposed the court 10 months before, was forced to vote against it.

Before the new World Court could begin to function, it had to be ratified by 60 nations. Some thought it might take 10 years or more to receive the necessary ratifications.

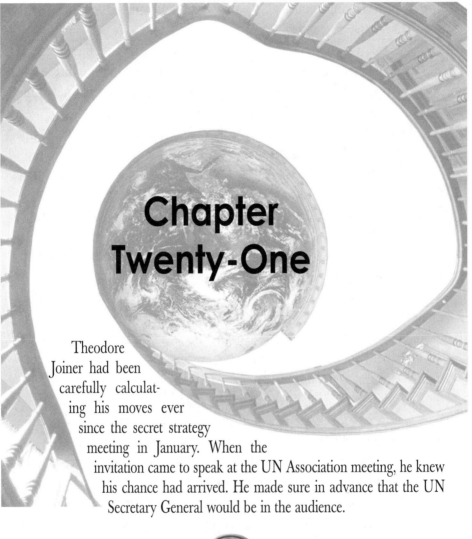

Chapter
Twenty-One

Theodore Joiner had been carefully calculating his moves ever since the secret strategy meeting in January. When the invitation came to speak at the UN Association meeting, he knew his chance had arrived. He made sure in advance that the UN Secretary General would be in the audience.

The UN's Robert Mahli introduced Joiner. "Ladies and gentlemen: We are very privileged to have a speaker today who has proven himself to be a true friend of global governance. He has generously donated his considerable talents, as well as his financial resources, toward the cause of global peace and security. It is with great pleasure that I present to you, Mr. Theodore Joiner."

"Thank you, Robert," Joiner responded. "Mr. Secretary General and distinguished guests, it's nice to be with you today in the little town of New York." Appreciative smiles were exchanged around the room. There was no one quite like Theodore Joiner.

Joiner continued, "I just happen to believe that everyone in this room is involved in the greatest project ever attempted by humankind." The audience broke into applause. "We live in the most dangerous time of all history–the nuclear age. Yet the United Nations has worked tirelessly to wage peace when some among us have been determined to wage war. To be honest, I'm not sure our world would still be in existence if it were not for the UN. So on behalf of my family and the entire world, I thank you.

"Now for the business at hand." Joiner paused looking around the room. "In spite of all the good that has been done, there are still monumental tasks yet to be accomplished. We are within reaching distance of a world structure of peace and security, yet we are still so far away. The shortsighted clinging to national sovereignty and religious exclusiveness still has the potential of plunging our world into the abyss of Armageddon.

"As we approach the new millennium, we must take the bold action necessary to lay these twin monsters to rest forever. The time has come to banish national and religious strife from the face of the earth once and for all. This critical challenge rests, first of all, upon the people in this room. Secondly, it rests upon the leaders of the world. Thirdly, it depends on every member of society. I have come to New York today to issue a new challenge to my fellow world citizens everywhere. The time has come for more than lip service. We need involvement at every level. It's time for each of us who have been blessed with financial means to put our money where our mouth is. Together, we really can build a new world order."

Joiner paused, taking in the face of every person in the crowd. At that moment, Robert Mahli remembered Joiner's words in the January strategy meeting, "I have a plan to join politics and religion together," he had said. Mahli realized that Joiner was getting ready to launch that plan right now.

"I propose that two great summits be held to launch the world into the new millennium," Joiner explained. "These should be held back to back at the UN. The first meeting, the Millennium Peace Summit, will be a meeting of one thousand of the top religious leaders from around the world." A ripple of heightened interest spread around the room at this proposal. There had never been a religious gathering at the UN since its founding.

Joiner plunged on. "Its purpose will be to convince these religious leaders that they must help build the new world order. They have the ears of the people. If they fight what we are attempting to do—which they have done many times, we will fail. When a new political initiative needs to be launched, key political leaders must communicate with key spiritual leaders. These spiritual leaders must then spread the word to all of their colleagues, who will in turn influence their followers around the world to support the steps being taken."

The Secretary General sat with a big smile on his face. Theodore Joiner was a maverick, but you didn't become a multi-billionaire by being stupid.

"The second meeting will be for the world's heads-of-state. It will simply be called the Millennium Summit. This will open the 55th General Assembly. At this meeting the Secretary General can present his plan for leading the world into the 21st Century.

"We will ask key religious leaders to stay over for the political summit so that relationships can be established with key political leaders for future cooperation." Spontaneous applause broke out all over the meeting room at Joiner's brilliant proposal.

Joiner went on. "Oh yes, there's one more thing. I am convinced that we stand right now at the crossroads of human history. I commit to you and to the world community that I will do everything in my power to see the plans I have outlined today are carried out.

"Being a businessman, I know these things take money. Mr. Secretary General and UN delegates, I am very happy today to present to the United Nations a gift of one billion dollars."

The audience sat for a moment in stunned silence. One billion dollars! Then suddenly all of the people rose to their feet in thunderous applause.

The Secretary General left his seat to personally thank Joiner for this unprecedented gesture. Then he took to the podium to respond. "Ladies and gentlemen: We have just witnessed true global citizenship in action. Theodore, I accept your plan and your challenge. It is brilliant. Needless to say, you will be the keynote speaker for the Millennium Peace Summit. Once again, on behalf of the world, I say thanks."

For the second time, the audience rose to its feet in sustained applause.

Chapter
Twenty-Two

Nego-
tiations at the
Kyoto environ-
mental conference
were not easy.
Requiring nations to take
actions which might adversely affect their economies was a
tough sell. This was especially difficult when no damaging
effects from the problem were expected for 75 years or more.

After long and tedious negotiations, the terms of the Kyoto Treaty were finalized. It was agreed that carbon dioxide emissions should be reduced to five percent below 1990 levels by 2012.

The easy part was done. Now the governments had to be convinced to ratify the treaty that was bound to alter every person's way of life. That promised to be an uphill battle.

When Michael first caught wind of possible problems with Y2K, he immediately sought more information. Anytime a problem of the magnitude that some of the articles were describing came along, there was tremendous opportunity to exploit those problems for the advancement of the New World Order.

Those warning of the problem explained that in the early days of computers, programmers had conserved precious memory space by only coding in the last two digits of the year instead of all four. They never dreamed that some of that code would still be in use by the turn of the century. Consequently, when the year 2000 rolled around, some were saying that the computers would not know whether the year was 1900 or 2000. They contended that insurance companies and financial institutions that depended on computers for their financial calculations would be thrown into utter chaos when their systems broke down on January 1, 2000.

Rumors swept the world that the computers controlling the production of electricity would malfunction, causing rolling blackouts that would take the world's power grids down for long periods of time. Of course, without electricity world business would come to a screeching halt. Life, as everyone had come to know it, would cease to exist.

In the articles that Michael had read, the cure was for all computers to be brought up-to-date, making them Y2K compliant. He saw in this problem a chance to remove one of the huge obstacles standing in the way of his world government plans.

You could not manage what you could not measure. Michael dreamed of a totally computerized society where the history of every business and every person would be available at the touch of a button. The problem was that many of the computer systems of the world were antiquated. He saw in Y2K the inducement to retire obsolete equipment, replacing it with the latest technology. "Yes, Y2K, true or not, will serve my purpose very well indeed," he thought to himself.

Arachev decided that Y2K was so important that the CEOs of the world's two largest computer firms should be invited to the 1998 insiders' planning session. When he suggested this to Morris Samuels, Morris objected, "Should these people be allowed access to the inner counsel of our network?"

Michael's reply came quickly, "You don't think these corporate leaders would have been allowed to control something as important to our future as the world's computer technology unless they themselves were part of the insider network, do you?"

"Are we at the point where we allow companies to succeed or fail on the basis of their feelings about the New World Order?"

"Definitely," Michael affirmed. "Morris, we are closer to our goal than most anyone realizes. The insiders' reach extends into almost every facet of human activity—colleges, financial institutions, big business, media, Hollywood, religion—everywhere. Notice to whom the big business tycoons make their donations. They give huge gifts to environmentalism, the United Nations, National Public Radio, key colleges in our network, and thousands of other globalist causes.

"Of course, it's best if the person has been raised in the right family," Michael explained. "In that case, everything evolves naturally since the belief system is already there. The proper ways of thinking are deeply engrained. But if that's not the case, the proper thinking can also be instilled through attending the right college."

Michael continued. "When individuals begin to reach the level of success where they can be an influence at the global level, they are invited to the 'right meetings' and introduced to the 'right people.' The message is subtly conveyed that if certain ways of thinking are adopted, doors to big finance and to large contracts will swing open. If the individual doesn't 'play the game,' those doors suddenly begin to close. You would be astounded at how quickly the political thinking of a person can change when they realize that reaching their dreams depends on it."

"So the CEOs of the two leading computer companies are firmly in our camp?" Morris inquired, wanting to be sure.

"No doubt about it," Michael asserted. "They have been tested and then tested again. They are reliable or else their businesses would not have been allowed to grow to their present levels."

When the first week of January came, the usual participants converged on San Francisco. The meeting was to be held at the former U.S. military base, the Presidio. Since its closing, it had become a center for one-world activities.

For the sake of the newcomers, Arachev made the introductions–starting around the room from his left: "My wife Rada." She nodded smiling. "Barbara and Morris Samuels, chairpersons of the Save the Earth Council.

Before Arachev had a chance to continue, Theodore Joiner, who was seated next to Morris, interrupted. "Hi. I'm Theodore, I'm this group's official boat rocker." Everyone laughed at Joiner being his usual unpredictable self.

"You certainly are," Michael responded. "I heard you rocked the United Nations' boat to the tune of $1 billion." Everyone in the room broke into enthusiastic applause.

Arachev continued the introductions. "Next to Theodore, of course, is our esteemed Secretary General of the United Nations.

"Next is Bill Baker with the World Federalist Movement." Bill nodded. "To Bill's left is Bishop James Hanscom, the driving force behind the future United Religions Organization.

"Next to Bishop Hanscom is my associate at Green Earth International, Simon Peters. Sitting next to him is Robert Mahli, Undersecretary General of the UN, and Alan Black, head of the World Bank.

"This is the first time for the next two gentlemen to be in attendance at our meeting. I have asked them to be with us for a very special reason. Please meet Byron Yates, the head of GlobalSoft International and Bradford Landry, CEO for Landry Computers, the world's number one computer manufacturer. It's wonderful to have these men with us, and I thank them for coming." The group welcomed them with a warm round of applause. Several people crossed the room to shake hands with the men personally.

When everyone was settled again, Arachev continued speaking, "As you know, this meeting usually consists of a spontaneous brainstorming session. However, there is an issue of such paramount importance we felt it should be at the top of our discussion list. There will certainly be time for our normal interaction later."

Theodore Joiner spoke up. "Michael, we're anxious to hear what you feel is so important."

Michael began, "How many of you have heard of Y2K?" Only a few had. "Some people are telling us that a glitch in our computer programming could result in the world shutting down when the computer clocks roll over to the year 2000. If this proves to be true, we will have a crisis of unprecedented proportions on our hands. Can you imagine it? Paychecks would not be delivered, food supplies would not be ordered, airline scheduling and reservations would come to a screeching halt. In short, total chaos would result.

"I've asked Byron and Bradford to explain this problem to us and to give us their ideas as to how we can exploit this crisis to accelerate movement into the New World Order. Byron is one of the leading experts on software and how it runs the world's computers. Byron..."

"Thanks for the invitation to be here, Michael," Byron began. "It is a pleasure to rub shoulders with such distinguished fellow globalists. I'm sure it goes without saying that whatever is said here must not be repeated outside of this room. This is especially critical concerning Y2K.

"Since GlobalSoft is the world's leading provider of computer operating systems, we have already been bombarded with questions about the potential problems of Y2K. As soon as the questions began to come, we had a meeting of our top people. It was agreed that no significant problems would occur because of the year 2000.

"However, at the same time, we realized we were being presented with an opportunity to upgrade computer systems, worldwide. We decided our stance should be that it's better to be safe than sorry. The message from our public relations department is that all software systems produced in 1998 or later can be trusted to be Y2K compliant.

"It was obvious to us that obsolete software could never be used to effectively connect the world into the coming interdependent global society. We anticipate that most businesses will totally update their computer hardware and software before the year 2000, just to be safe.

"Bradford, at this time I will turn it over to you."

"Thanks Byron," Bradford began. "Landry Computers and GlobalSoft work hand in hand. The GlobalSoft operating system is installed on every computer sold by Landry.

"We have adopted the same policy at Landry that Byron described to you. Already sales are escalating. We anticipate an almost total restructuring of the world's computer systems within the next two years. This will obviously present lucrative opportunities to computer companies everywhere. However, that is not what is important to us in this room today.

"The critical issue at hand is to effectively connect the world to the Internet. Once every human being on earth is connected, our global government will have complete access to all information worldwide. Then, and only then, will we be able to instantly identify those elements resisting our New World Order.

"Furthermore, once all businesses are online, we can move the world into a cashless, electronic economy. Any rebellious elements that will not fall in line with our global ethic can be punished by placing them under individual economic sanctions. We can then control what they are permitted to buy, if anything at all."

Theodore Joiner spoke up, "So we could place individuals under economic sanctions just as the UN places nations under economic sanctions to punish them and bring them into compliance.

"Exactly," Landry responded.

"What if it is found out that Y2K is nothing but a red herring? Couldn't this have negative repercussions on the government and the computer companies?" Bill Baker of the World Federalists asked.

"It won't happen," Yates assured. "The only people that understand computers well enough to know that Y2K is a hoax are the people running the computer companies. They are going to be making such incredible fortunes from all the upgrades that they won't dare kill the goose laying the golden egg."

"And if some voices do claim that the alarm is fraudulent, we will use our control of the media to isolate them," Samuels declared.

Finally, Bishop Hanscom said what everyone was silently thinking, "But this deception is going to cost the world hundreds of billions of dollars. We've admitted that Y2K is not going to happen. Do we have a right to perpetrate this deception upon the world?"

Michael Arachev never blinked. "Ladies and gentlemen, this world is headed for destruction without our New World Order. We are not exploiting anyone with this decision. We are facilitating the very thing that will ultimately save them. What's a few billion dollars when the future of the world hangs in the balance? What we are deciding here today is for the common good of humankind." At Arachev's forceful words, heads around the room nodded in agreement. The decision was made.

For the remainder of the meeting, Bishop Hanscom reported on the progress of the charter for the United Religions Organization. Theodore Joiner explained the plans that were being made for the religious and political Millennium Summits that would take place in 2000. Bill Baker informed everyone of the steps being taken for the birth of the International Criminal Court.

But, without a doubt, the big news of the insiders' 1998 strategy session was using the Y2K crisis to update the computers of the world in preparation for the coming interconnected, interdependent global society.

Chapter Twenty-Three

Plans were being meticulously laid for the two summits that would launch the world into the 21st Century. The one-worlders were counting heavily on the success of these meetings.

Theodore Joiner had hired Stanford Jackson as chairman of the World Hope Foundation, which had been set up to administer the one billion dollar donation he had made to the UN. He and Jackson had worked together toward globalist causes for many years. Jackson knew his way around the one-world crowd as well as anyone.

Jackson and Joiner worked very closely together while planning the religious summit. The religious leaders on the invitation list were screened one by one. All names were subjected to certain criteria: Did the individuals think globally? Were they tolerant and respectful of other religions? Were they well-connected politically? And most importantly, did they enjoy a wide sphere of influence among their religious peers?

Once the plans for the religious summit were completed, Joiner met with the UN Secretary General to review them. The Secretary was pleased with the guest list. Everything appeared to be in order.

Before leaving, Joiner reminded the Secretary General, "The success of this meeting rises or falls on getting those in attendance to sign a declaration supporting the UN's efforts toward world peace. Once they sign it, they own it. They will then feel duty-bound to defend it."

"I'm in agreement with you," the Secretary General assured. "But what kind of statement do we want them to sign?"

Joiner paused for a moment. "Why don't I contact Michael Arachev? You know, he's very good at crafting statements that will tie people into globalism without unduly alarming them."

"Excellent," the Secretary General replied. "Let me know what he comes up with."

Not being one to let grass grow under his feet, Joiner was in Arachev's office the next morning.

Michael knew there was something very important pending. Joiner would not have called for an appointment on such short notice unless the matter was urgent. Fortunately, Michael was able to shift his schedule to accomodate him.

"Good morning, Theodore!" Michael exclaimed as his secretary showed Joiner into the room.

"Michael, great to see you!" Joiner said with warm enthusiasm. "Thanks for making time to receive such an itinerant one-worlder as myself on such short notice." They both laughed at Joiner's reckless candor.

"Sit down, Theodore," Michael urged, motioning to one of the chairs beside the fireplace. "Coffee?"

"I think I will," Theodore accepted. "It's brisk outside this morning."

Once settled, Joiner moved immediately to the business at hand. "I've just come from meeting with the Secretary General. We've been discussing the Millennium Peace Summit of the World's Religious Leaders. I attempted to impress upon the Secretary General the importance of not just having a meeting. It's my opinion that we must get the religious leaders to sign on to a unifying statement of purpose before they leave New York. Without that, I think the meeting will do very little good. But if we can get a statement from the top one thousand religious leaders of the world, it will be of tremendous value to the global cause."

Michael responded immediately, "I agree. What kind of statement do you have in mind?"

"Well, that's why I'm here," Joiner explained. "The Secretary General and I thought that you would be the ideal person to draft the statement. No one can express our global agenda, without making it sound like one, quite as skillfully as you can."

Michael smiled. "Flattery will get you everywhere," he said, letting Joiner know that he understood he was being cajoled.

"So you'll do it?" Theodore asked, already knowing the answer. Michael never turned down any job, no matter how difficult, if it would further his dream of global government.

"When do you need it?" Michael inquired.

"We'll need it in time to go over it with the Secretary General. As you know, he will be a key player in selling it to the delegates. We will also want to share it with the key leaders of the major religions in advance. If we get all of them on board prior to the meeting, they will have prepared their constituents before the summit.

"Could you have it in a month?" Joiner asked.

"I'll do my best," Michael agreed. "You know that an effort like this requires inspiration. Sometimes it's there, and sometimes it's not. I'll contact you as soon as I've finished."

In less than a month, the document entitled "Commitment to Global Peace" was completed. Arachev mailed the final draft to Theodore Joiner with considerable satisfaction. He felt he had succeeded in producing a statement of principles that would pull the religious leaders of the world into the global agenda.

When Joiner received Arachev's work, he read it immediately.

THE MILLENNIUM WORLD PEACE SUMMIT OF RELIGIOUS AND SPIRITUAL LEADERS

Commitment to Global Peace
Humanity stands at a critical juncture in history, one that calls for strong moral and spiritual leadership to help set a new direction for society. We, as religious and spiritual leaders, recognize our unique responsibility for the well-being of the human family and peace on earth.

Whereas the United Nations and the religions of the world have a common concern for human dignity, justice and peace;

Whereas we accept that men and women are equal partners in all aspects of life, and children are the hope of the future;

Whereas religions have contributed to the peace of the world but have also been used to create division and fuel hostilities;

Whereas our world is plagued by violence, war and destruction, which are sometimes perpetrated in the name of religion;

Whereas armed conflict is a dire tragedy for the human lives ruined and lost, for the larger living world, and for the future of our religious and spiritual traditions;

Whereas no individual, group or nation can continue to live as an isolated microcosm in our interdependent world, but rather all must realize that our every action has an impact on others and the emerging global community;

Whereas in an interdependent world, peace requires agreement on fundamental ethical values;

Whereas there can be no real peace until all groups and communities acknowledge the cultural and religious diversity of the human family in a spirit of mutual respect and understanding; Whereas building peace requires an attitude of reverence for life, freedom and justice, the eradication of poverty, and the protection of the environment for present and future generations;

Whereas a true culture of peace must be founded upon the cultivation of the inner dimension of peace, which is the heritage of the religious and spiritual traditions;

Whereas religious and spiritual traditions are a core source of the realization of a better life for the human family and all life on Earth.

In light of the above, and with a view to discharging our duty to the human family, we declare our commitment and determination:

1. To collaborate with the United Nations and all men and women of goodwill locally, regionally and globally in the pursuit of peace in all its dimensions;

2. To lead humanity by word and deed in a renewed commitment to ethical and spiritual values, which include a deep sense of respect for all life and for each person's inherent dignity and right to live in a world free of violence;

3. To manage and resolve nonviolently the conflicts generated by religious and ethnic differences, and to condemn all violence committed in the name of religion while seeking to remove the roots of the violence;

4. To appeal to all religious communities and ethnic and national groups to respect the right to freedom of religion, to seek reconciliation, and to engage in mutual forgiveness and healing;

5. To awaken in all individuals and communities a sense of shared responsibility for the well-being of the human family as a whole, and a recognition that all human beings, regardless of religion, race, gender and ethnic origin have the right to education, health care, and an opportunity to achieve a secure and sustainable livelihood;

6. To promote the equitable distribution of wealth within nations and among nations, eradicating poverty and reversing the current trend toward a widening gap between rich and poor;

7. To educate our communities about the urgent need to care for the earth's ecological systems and all forms of life, and to support efforts to make environmental protection and restoration integral to all developmental planning and activity;

8. To join with the United Nations in the call for all nation states to work for the universal abolition of nuclear weapons and other weapons of mass destruction for the safety and security of life on this planet;

9. To practice and promote in our communities the values of the inner dimension of peace, including study, prayer, meditation, a sense of the sacred, humility, love, compassion, tolerance, and a spirit of service, which are fundamental to the creation of a peaceful society.

We, as religious and spiritual leaders, pledge our commitment to work together to promote the inner and outer conditions that foster peace and the nonviolent management and resolution of conflict. We appeal to the followers of all religious traditions and to the human community as a whole to cooperate in building peaceful societies, to seek mutual understanding through dialogue where there are differences, to refrain from violence, to practice compassion, and to uphold the dignity of all life.

Joiner went over the Peace Declaration with great satisfaction and admiration. No one could say it quite like Michael Arachev. The principles of the New World Order were all there.

- *No individual, group or nation can continue to live isolated in our interdependent world.*
- *Our every action has an impact on others and the emerging global community.*
- *In an interdependent world, peace requires agreement on fundamental ethical values.*
- *All groups and communities must acknowledge the cultural and religious diversity of the human family in a spirit of mutual respect and understanding.*
- *Building peace requires an attitude of reverence for life, the eradication of poverty, and the protection of the environment for present and future generations.*
- *Everyone must promote the equitable distribution of wealth within nations and among nations.*
- *Commitment to environmentalism.*
- *All must collaborate with the United Nations.*

When Joiner next met with the UN Secretary General, he went over the "Commitment to Global Peace" with him. "This is wonderful," the Secretary exclaimed. "Everything is here. I wouldn't change a thing."

The UN General Assembly Hall had never witnessed a scene quite like the opening session of the Millennium Peace Summit of Religious and Spiritual Leaders. The room was filled with Sikh turbans; the black robes of Muslims; magenta garments of Catholic priests; red robes of Catholic cardinals; Sufi hats; and the ornate Eagle headdresses of Native Americans. Mixed in were the white bonnets of the Russian Orthodox Church; the purple robes of African priests; and the feather headdresses on those from Brazil and Central America...just to mention a few.

At 9:25 a.m., the official opening of the Assembly began with Traditional African Drums by Baba Olatunji. The African dancers came onto the stage swirling and dancing in their native costumes. As the ceremony progressed, the drums grew louder, and the dancers moved more vigorously. When the frantic activity reached its highest peak, the drumbeat stopped just as suddenly as it had started.

The Secretary General for the Millennium Peace Summit was Anwar Singh. He stepped up to the podium to give his opening address.

"Honorable and distinguished delegates, we, the religious leaders of the world, are gathered here at the United Nations to foster a climate of peace among the peoples of the world.

"Increasingly, the responsibility for finding solutions to global problems, as well as regional conflicts, is falling to the United Nations. Although essentially a political body, the United Nations has had, since its inception, strong spiritual underpinnings.

"Many years ago, Secretary-General Dag Hammarskjöld said, 'We have tried to make peace on this earth, and we have failed miserably. Unless there is a spiritual renaissance, this world will know no peace.'

"It was the dream of another distinguished Secretary-General, U Thant, a deeply spiritual man, to see a convergence of the political and spiritual.

"And now, at the turn of the millennium, with the support of our present Secretary-General, religious leaders from around the world are gathered at the United Nations Headquarters for the first time in the organization's fifty-five-year history.

"During our time together, we will be exploring how our religious and political institutions can work in partnership to secure greater peace.

"Let this Summit be the beginning of our efforts to strengthen the work of the United Nations around the globe, and to bring greater spiritual leadership to its endeavors.

"Thank you, and welcome to New York."

Singh's welcome was followed by a prayer given by His Eminence Sheikh Ahmed Kuftaro, the Islamic Grand Mufti of Syria.

Anwar Singh then returned to the podium. "Thank you so much, Sheikh Kuftaro. Now, ladies and gentlemen, it is with great pleasure that I introduce to you the Secretary General of the United Nations."

The religious leaders greeted him with a standing ovation. It was clear they wanted to hear what the leader of the UN had to say.

"Ladies and gentlemen, thank you so much for answering the call to bring your spiritual influence to the center of global governance–the United Nations.

"I want to say to you in no uncertain terms that there must be no room in the 21st century for religious bigotry and intolerance. I urge you, as religious leaders in our world, to set an example of interfaith dialogue and cooperation.

"You can help bridge the chasms of ignorance, fear and misunderstanding, as teachers and guides; you can be powerful agents of change. You can inspire people to new levels of commitment and public service.

"I must remind you that, although religion should be equated with light, too often its practice has displayed its darker side. Religious extremism has, at many times, oppressed or discriminated against women and minorities. Religion has often been yoked to nationalism, stoking the flames of violent conflict and setting group against group.

"To look out over this gathering of leaders representing seventy-five different religions is one of the most inspiring experiences I have enjoyed as Secretary General.

"Now I call upon you–I urge you–to rise to the challenge of this summit. Let us all look within ourselves and determine to do everything within our power to promote justice, equality, reconciliation and peace."

The Secretary General returned to his place at the head table to a loud and sustained ovation.

As soon as the delegates were seated, music from a flute began wafting through the Assembly Hall. From the wing stepped Native American, Frank Menusan, playing a haunting Native American worship melody.

At the conclusion of the song, Anwar Singh commented, "That was very enriching and inspiring. Thank you, Frank."

Singh continued, "Our next speaker is no stranger to any of us. This is the man who conceived the idea of this religious peace summit here at the UN. He is an avid supporter of the UN and its pursuit of peace, and he puts his money where his mouth is. This good man has funded this entire conference, including the expenses of each delegate. Please make welcome, ladies and gentlemen, Mr. Theodore Joiner."

Immediately, the delegates rose to their feet in thunderous applause. The reception for the Secretary General had been strong and polite. The welcome for Joiner was excited and enthusiastic.

"Well, thank you very much," Joiner began. "It's great to see all of you.

"I've been dreaming of a conference like this for many years. When I was a little boy, I was very religious. I was born into a Christian family and went to a Christian school. I became a Christian the way you become whatever you're exposed to as a little child. I was going to be a man of the cloth. I would have been sitting out there with you, and I would have loved that life. I was going to be a missionary. First I studied Christianity, but later I started studying the world's great religions and that made me think.

"What disturbed me was the intolerance of my Christian sect—not intolerance towards others' religious freedom. But they believed we were the only people going to Heaven. The Catholics weren't going to Heaven, and neither were Protestants, Jews, Muslims, Hindus or Buddhists. Nobody was going to Heaven but us! And there were only a few of us...perhaps less than one percent of the world's population. It confused me. I thought, 'Heaven will be a very empty place with nobody else there.' I realized it couldn't be right. That caused me to spend more time studying and thinking.

"Finally, within the last ten or twenty years, I have gotten to know Native Americans. There is a lot to be learned from indigenous people. After all, they were here for millions of years. There are many different languages, forms of music, dances and cultures, but basically we are all the same. We love our children. We love our wives, our husbands. We love our religions. We love the same things. So I reasoned that maybe, instead of all these different gods, there's one God who manifests Himself and reveals Himself in different ways to different people.

"When most of the great religions were started thousands of years ago, people didn't travel. We lived in little enclaves, and what we did didn't affect other people. We could afford to have fights with each other. Most of the fights in those days were limited to fists, like prize-fights. You beat someone up, then you helped him up, and that was the end of it. There were no weapons of mass destruction.

"In World War II, people still thought there was more than one race of man. There was the white race, the black race, the yellow race, and the red man. Remember, Hitler thought that there was an Aryan race. Scientists and archeologists have demonstrated that we are just one human race. And we all originated from Africa and spread out over the world. We have different colors because the white people lived in the North, and the dark people lived in the South just as bears in the North are white and bears in the South are black. Yet, they are still bears.

"So, we are all one race, and there is only one God who manifests Himself in different ways. The religions that have survived are the ones that are built on love. What we have to do now is work together. A lot of terrible things have been done in the name of religion in the past, and we can't afford it anymore. Now we have nuclear weapons, poison gas, land mines and aerial bombardment, and the world is not safe.

"It's time to get rid of hatred and prejudice. It's time to have love and respect and tolerance for each other, care about each other, and work together to survive. I think God wants us to love each other, live in peace and harmony and figure out how to solve the horrible, grinding problems of poverty, to have a more equitable, fairer, kinder, more peaceful, gentle, loving world.

"I'm convinced that you sitting in front of me are the key to bringing the dream of peace to reality. You speak to your followers on a consistent basis. You impart your values to them. Together, we can create a culture of peace. We can produce a world where love conquers hate.

"As one mere human being who cares what happens to my children and my grandchildren and to yours, I ask you to join me in sending a

141

message to this world. Let our voice from this summit be heard around the world. Let the world hear our unified declaration of peace.

"I'm asking for a commitment to peace here tonight from every religious leader. If you will commit to peace on earth, stand to your feet right now."

Every delegate in the UN Assembly Hall stood quickly. Spontaneously the applause began—the crescendo growing stronger until it felt as though the walls were beginning to vibrate. Some of the African delegation began to beat their drums and broke into dancing. All over the Assembly Hall, men and women were clapping their hands and stomping their feet. It could only be described as a singular moment in UN history.

The celebration continued for a full 10 minutes. Joiner and the Secretary General watched the jubilation with smiles on their faces. Finally, Joiner stepped back to the podium, raising his hands to quiet the audience. The delegates quickly fell silent, wanting to hear what else Joiner had to say.

"Please be seated for one more moment," Joiner requested. Once the delegates were seated, he continued, "We have one last piece of unfinished business. We came here from all over the world because we mean business. I'm asking the ushers to pass out a copy of our Commitment to Global Peace Declaration. This declaration has been printed in duplicate. The top copy is for you to take home with you. The second copy is for you to sign and turn in.

"Allow me to summarize the principles contained in this Commitment to Global Peace:

- *No individual, group or nation can continue to live isolated in our interdependent world.*
- *Our every action has an impact on others and the emerging global community.*
- *In an interdependent world, peace requires agreement on fundamental ethical values.*

- *All groups and communities must acknowledge the cultural and religious diversity of the human family in a spirit of mutual respect and understanding.*
- *Building peace requires an attitude of reverence for life, the eradication of poverty, and the protection of the environment for present and future generations.*
- *Everyone must promote the equitable distribution of wealth within nations and among nations.*
- *Commitment to environmentalism.*
- *All must collaborate with the United Nations.*

"As soon as you sign the Peace Declaration, the ushers will come by to collect them. Once again, thank you very much."

After the signed commitments were gathered up, the Summit was adjourned until the next day. Delegates stood in small groups for over an hour discussing the evening's inspiring events.

The remainder of the Peace Summit featured such outstanding religious leaders as: Cardinal Jacques Azinger, President of the Vatican's Pontifical Council for Interreligious Dialogue; the Grand Mufti of Bosnia, Bostafa Hamric; Israeli Chief Rabbi Josef Rikin; the Rev. James Manson; and evangelist Marilyn Hightower. But the highpoint of the meeting was definitely the speech by Theodore Joiner.

At the conclusion of the Summit, all delegates stood facing outward. They were asked to stretch out their arms and bestow a blessing upon the world. After the mass prayer, the McCullough Sons of Thunder concluded the Summit with a rousing rendition of "United House of Prayer for All People." The delegates disbursed with a sense of euphoria. Surely, the world would never be the same.

Joiner and the globalists had what they wanted: signed commitments to their global agenda from the world's top religious leaders. All that remained was the establishment of the Religious Liaison Committee that would work with the United Nations. Those committee members would be handpicked by Joiner, Jackson and the UN Secretary General. They would make sure that those individuals would be committed globalists

Chapter
Twenty-Four

All 189 member-states of the United Nations were present when the Millennium Summit convened on September 6, 2000. Out of the 189 delegates from the world's nations, 150 were heads-of-state. It was the largest meeting of its kind in the history of the world. A pivotal time like this only came about every 1,000 years. There was definitely a feeling of history in the making as the world leaders filed into the UN Assembly Hall to plan for the new millennium.

The Millennium Summit's agenda was filled with speeches by each of the heads-of-state. Each leader was allotted five minutes. The highlight of the Summit was the speech given by the Secretary General.

"Mr. President, Excellencies, ladies and gentlemen, I have a distinct sense of destiny as I stand before you this day. I don't think it is a coincidence that the first true structures of global governance have fallen into place in time to enter the new age of the new millennium.

"We have the United Nations that has been so carefully built by my predecessors and the leaders of the world over the last fifty-five years. More recently, the World Trade Organization, the International Monetary Fund and the many other arms of the World Community have begun to function as they were intended.

"Now, as we stand on the brink of the next thousand years, the uniting of the world's religions is in progress. At the same time, the new world court system will soon be ratified making international law enforceable.

"All of these developments beckon us to enter the promised land of global peace and security. Can we beat our swords into plowshares and our spears into pruning hooks? Can we disarm the world and leave the terrible scourge of war behind us forever? I think we can. The bigger question that each of us must ask is—will we?

"Do we even have a choice? When one billion people are attempting to live on less than $1 per day, can we afford not to unite? When clean water and proper sanitation is no longer available to a large portion of our population, can we ignore it—hoping the problem will simply go away? Lastly, greenhouse gas emissions are eating away at the atmosphere that is essential for sustaining life. Will we bequeath to our children and grandchildren a world that is uninhabitable? Unless we exchange our irresponsible patterns of consumption for sustainable growth patterns and development, we will.

"Do we have the courage to make the difficult decisions as we peer into the new millennium? Will it be a promised land or a no-man's land for mankind?

"We have the necessary structures for global governance. Let's empower the organizations we have created so that they can become the instruments of global peace and security. Let's embrace the Kyoto Treaty so that our descendants will have clean air to breathe and clean water to drink.

"Ladies and gentlemen—we must do this! Do we have a choice? The Global Forum, held earlier this year, has hammered out a document that will serve as the roadmap into the new millennium. It is called the Millennium Declaration. You were provided with a copy of the Declaration in advance of this meeting. As I stand before you today, I urge this Summit to adopt the Millennium Declaration.

"Adopting it will unify us. It will allow us to work together as never before. It will provide a shining light for the human race as we enter the murky, uncharted waters of the 21st century.

"If you, the leaders of the world, will join me in embracing the future of humankind, I ask you to vote for the adoption of the Millennium Declaration by standing with me now."

All 189 delegates rose to their feet as one. The vote was unanimous. The united mind of the world's leadership was inspiring to witness. The feeling that pervaded the UN General Assembly Hall could only be described as euphoric!

The Millennium Declaration was not the exact same document as the Commitment to Global Peace that the world's religious leaders had signed one week earlier, but each of the documents contained the same principles.

The Millennium Declaration included the following:

- **International law:** *The only road to world peace is through international law.*
- **Wealth redistribution:** *Equality of all people must be facilitated through redistribution of the world's wealth from the "have" nations to the "have nots."*
- **Tolerance**—*All beliefs, cultures and religions should be respected. Differences within and between societies should be neither feared nor repressed, but cherished as a precious asset of humanity.*
- **Culture of peace:** *A culture of peace must be fostered in all the world's inhabitants from the very beginning of life. This new way of thinking must be carefully taught throughout the educational process.*

- *Sustainable development: Prudence must be shown in the management of all living species and natural resources, in accordance with the precepts of sustainable development. The current unsustainable patterns of production and consumption must be changed in the interest of our future welfare and that of our descendants.*

- *Kyoto Protocol: We must make every effort to ensure the entry into force of the Kyoto Protocol, preferably by the tenth anniversary of the United Nations Conference on Environment and Development in 2002, and to embark on the required reduction in emissions of greenhouse gases.*

- *Develop the world court system: Strengthen the International Court of Justice, in order to ensure justice and the rule of law in international affairs.*

- *Support for the UN: We solemnly reaffirm, on this historic occasion, that the United Nations is the indispensable common house of the entire human family, through which we will seek to realize our universal aspirations for peace, cooperation and development. We therefore pledge our unstinting support for these common objectives and our determination to achieve them.*

As the delegates left New York, each one understood that the world had been given its marching orders.

Chapter
Twenty-Five

The insiders' annual strategy meeting normally alternated locations between the Presidio and the Samuels' ranch. This year they headed back to the ranch. Breakfast on the first morning was simply wonderful. The coffee was hot. The orange juice and milk were ice cold. The meal included eggs, bacon, sausage, hash browns–crisp but not burnt, and biscuits and gravy. By the time breakfast was over, everyone was in a good mood.

In the conference room, Rada and Barbara were given the two seats closest to the warm, radiant fire. The Secretary General took a seat far away from the heat. Too much warmth and he became sleepy. He didn't want to doze off during this important meeting.

Michael plunged right in. "Theodore, tell us about the Millennium World Peace Summit. How did it go?"

"It was terrific," Joiner reported. "The religious leaders signed on to the Commitment for Global Peace, and the political leaders unanimously approved the Millennium Declaration. As you know, these two documents contain the same principles, only stated in a little different way.

"Now we are in the process of setting up the liaison between the religious leaders and the United Nations. It will be called the World Council of Religious Leaders. We are on our way to making it fully functional."

The Secretary General spoke up, "Theodore's speech was masterful. He said what most of the religious delegates were already thinking. I have to say that the meeting far exceeded my expectations. Before he was done, he had every one of them clapping their hands, stomping their feet and dancing in the aisles. It was like being at a charismatic revival!" the Secretary laughed.

"An alliance between politics and religion will open the door to true global unity," Arachev stated confidently. "Theodore, you may have accomplished the greatest breakthrough toward the New World Order in the last fifty years. Great job!" Everyone in the room applauded.

Bill Baker of the World Federalists spoke up. "I suppose everyone has heard by now that the President of the United States did sign the International Criminal Court Statute. That's very good news, even though it was done on the last possible day."

"Why did he fight it for so long, Bill?" Theodore Joiner inquired.

Baker explained, "The President understands that this is an instrument of global governance that he will not be able to control since the U.S. has no veto power over the Court. He realizes this is the most dramatic erosion of national sovereignty since the UN was formed. That's why he was so reluctant to sign. However, he didn't want the U.S. to be left without a say in the Court's future development. So in the end, he signed."

"How long will it be until this World Court officially takes power?" Joiner asked.

All eyes in the room turned to Morris Samuels. He was the expert when it came to the functioning of UN operations. Morris began to explain, "When sixty national parliaments have ratified the ICC, it will become international law. At the present rate of ratification, the process could take up to ten years. However, if some kind of global crisis occurs, the ratification might be completed much sooner."

"This may be a foolish question," Joiner interrupted, "but who decided that sixty ratifications would bring this world court to power? There are one hundred-ninety nations in the UN, so fifty percent plus one would require ninety-six ratifications. How did the ICC Conference settle on sixty?"

Samuels explained, "The writers of the ICC Statute knew that securing ninety-six ratifications might be impossible. Therefore, a decision was made that once half of the nations voting for the ICC at Rome ratified, the international court would assume power."

Joiner questioned further in amazement, "Once sixty nations decide to impose a world court on the world's one hundred-ninety nations, it becomes international law binding on every nation on earth? Sixty nations can exercise power over the other one hundred-thirty nations against their will? How does the UN get away with it?"

The Secretary General spoke up. "Theodore, you have to understand the politics of the world. Most world leaders and UN ambassadors favor world government. Yet the people they represent are largely opposed to surrendering their sovereignty to the coming New World Order. Therefore, the world leaders know what is going on and are glad to allow it to happen. They can get the world government that they favor while voting against it. Thus, they do not raise the ire of their people. At the same time, the masses that oppose world government never look into what is going on behind the scenes, and don't realize how these things are being done. The few that do are ignored by the mainstream media; as a result, they have no appreciable effect on the outcome."

"It's like this, Theodore," Samuels interjected, "we in this room know that without the implementation of a world government, humankind will destroy themselves. Therefore, we have an obligation to do whatever it takes to save the masses from inevitable destruction, whether or not they agree with it."

"Interesting!" Joiner commented, raising his eyebrows with a smile.

Morris Samuels turned to Arachev, "Michael, what do you see as the critical developments that we should be working toward during this year?"

It was obvious that Michael was well prepared for the question. "There have been many important developments during the last few years," he began. "The formation of the United Religions was a major achievement. The Millennium Peace Summit and the Millennium Summit were huge successes. The acceptance of the Millennium Declaration as the global agenda was critical. The marriage of politics and religion was essential to the world's future.

"As we predicted last year, Y2K was a non-event. However, it served to mandate the upgrade of the world's computer systems. That will be vital as we implement a system for the efficient management of the world.

"All of the pieces of our New World Order are pretty much in place. We must now simply develop and perfect them. Implementation may seem slow right now, but when a world crisis comes–and there will be one–we will be able to accelerate dramatically.

"Our plan should be to achieve the ratification of the ICC and continue establishing the liaison between world political leaders and world religious leaders. The development of international law must continue as rapidly as possible. Implementation of the Kyoto Treaty must be aggressively promoted. Without this, our main instrument of wealth redistribution and international control over the U.S. will be thwarted.

"As each of us works in our particular spheres, world events will create opportunities that we cannot predict today. But rest assured they will happen. They always do."

Chapter Twenty-Six

Michael and Rada boarded the plane to Israel with great anticipation. The unexpected invitation had come from Israel's Peace Institute, and had been hand delivered by Israel's ambassador to the UN.

The peace prize they wanted to bestow on Michael was in recognition for the large number of Jews that he had allowed to leave the Soviet Union under his presidency.

When the plane touched down on the tarmac at Ben Gurion International Airport, Rada looked out the window. "So this is the Promised Land," she thought to herself. It looked like any other land, yet Rada found herself wondering if any of the legends surrounding this special place could possibly be true.

Michael and Rada were met at the airport by the Israeli Foreign Minister, Yosef Dore, and by officials from the Peace Institute. As they traveled from Tel Aviv to Jerusalem, Arachev's eyes drank in the historic land. He noted with interest the bustling modern city of Tel Aviv. But he was filled with anticipation for his first glimpse of Jerusalem.

Darkness had settled by the time they reached the outskirts of the Holy City. As they approached the city, Arachev was not prepared for what he saw. The walls around the Old City of Jerusalem were strategically spotlighted to emphasize their splendor. Rounding a curve, the Arachevs caught their first stunning glimpse of the Temple Mount. The awesome sight of the Dome of the Rock with its lighted gold dome against the darkened sky was like no other sight on earth. "It's beautiful!" Rada exclaimed.

"Is the location of the Dome of the Rock on the same site where the First and Second Jewish Temples stood?" Arachev asked the Foreign Minister.

"No one knows for sure," Dore replied. "Some contend it is the very place, and therefore the Dome of the Rock must come down. Others believe the Temples stood north of the Dome of the Rock in the large open area that you see there."

When their motorcade arrived at the King David Hotel, Arachev was reminded of all the kings and presidents who had stayed in this famous hotel in years past. Before leaving Michael and Rada for the night, Foreign Minister Dore promised to personally escort them around Jerusalem the next day.

At eight o'clock the next morning, Rada and Michael stepped into the Mercedes limousine provided by the Israeli government. Michael greeted their host, "Good morning Mr. Foreign Minister. It's so kind of you to take your valuable time to show us around the Holy Land."

"It's my pleasure, I assure you," Dore replied. Their limousine wound its way through the streets of Jerusalem, moving in the direction of the Mount of Olives.

They stepped out of their vehicle to see the Mount of Olives lookout with its breathtaking view. From where they were standing, the Temple Mount with the Al Aqsa Mosque and the Dome of the Rock were perhaps a block away, just across the Kidron Valley.

Josef Dore began his explanations. "I brought you here first because you can see the entire city of Jerusalem from this place. The New Testament teaches that it was from the Mount of Olives that Jesus prophesied the destruction of the Second Temple. He actually said that not one stone would be left upon another. Of course, the Temple was totally destroyed by the Romans a few years later in Seventy A.D. It was also from here that Jesus made His triumphal entry through the Golden Gate that you see across the way. That happened one week before He was crucified.

"Over to the right, down below is the Garden of Gethsemane where Jesus prayed into the night. It was there His betrayal by Judas took place."

As Michael listened to the words of the Foreign Minister, he attempted to comprehend what went through the mind of Christ during those fateful days. His actions in this very area had impacted the world and changed it forever. A feeling of strange resentment rose up within Arachev toward this Jesus who claimed to be the Messiah.

"You failed," Michael thought, mentally addressing Jesus. "You claimed to be the Prince of Peace, but there has been nothing but war since You left the earth. I will not fail. I will bring true peace to the human race."

"Michael, Michael!" Rada's voice finally pierced through the vivid thoughts captivating his mind. "Michael. Are you all right?" Rada asked with considerable concern.

"Yes. Yes, I'm fine," Michael replied apologetically. "I was just trying to drink in the historic impact of this place. How long were you waiting on me?"

"It was only about ten minutes," Rada answered. "It's all right."

The rest of the day was spent visiting the Western Wall, the Temple Mount and the Garden Tomb. After being inside the tomb, Arachev told himself, "It means nothing. It's a myth. I know He didn't rise from the dead." Still, the tomb was empty. It haunted him the rest of the day.

When it was evening, Foreign Minister Dore asked, "Are you ready to return to the hotel?"

Michael replied quickly, "I have a request."

"What is it?" Dore asked anxiously. "We want you to be able to do whatever you would like."

"Would it be possible for you to take me back by the Temple Mount?" Arachev requested. "And could I be left alone there for a little while?"

"Why certainly," Dore replied immediately. "We'll go right now."

"No," Michael responded quickly. "Drop Rada off at the King David. I'd like to be there alone, and I don't want to keep you any longer."

"That would be fine I am sure, Mr. Arachev," Dore answered. "However, my government would severely frown upon me if I left you totally without protection. I'm sure you can understand that."

"Yes. Certainly," Michael replied quickly. "If the bodyguards could keep watch from a distance, that would be fine. I'll try not to be too long."

Dore bid the Arachevs good night, and Rada returned to the room. The limousine turned back toward the Temple Mount.

Dore had called ahead, making all the necessary arrangements with the Wakf, the Muslim authority that administered the Temple Mount. By the time they arrived back at the entrance, the Muslim authorities were expecting him.

"Come in, Mr. Arachev. Welcome," the head Caliph greeted him warmly.

"Thank you for extending this courtesy to me," Arachev responded. "I won't be long."

"It's all right," the Caliph assured. "Take all the time you would like."

With the security detail following far behind, Arachev moved slowly across the stones of the Temple Mount floor. It seemed as though his sensibilities were suddenly heightened. He felt the history of the place and the struggles that had transpired here. He had the distinct impression of being surrounded by the forces of destiny.

Michael was strangely drawn to the southeast portion of the Temple Mount. Standing right in the corner, he was able to take in the incredible view. Looking to the extreme left, he saw the Dome of the Rock. Looking at a 90-degree angle to his left, he saw the Kidron Valley. To the right of the Kidron was the Garden of Gethsemane. Then straight-ahead was the ascent to the Mount of Olives.

Earlier in the day, Josef Dore had explained to him that it was on this pinnacle that the temptation of Jesus had taken place. It was here that Satan had come to Him, offering Him the kingdoms of the world. As Arachev rehearsed these things in his mind, the wind picked up velocity, whipping through his hair. A thought presented itself to his mind, "If Satan had offered you your long-dreamed-of world government, what would you have done?"

Michael rolled the proposition around in his mind. "I can't see that Jesus made the right decision. There's been nothing but war and more war ever since," he thought to himself.

The longer Arachev dwelt on these things, the more plausible the proposition seemed. Michael couldn't tell exactly when it happened, but at some point the experience took the form of reality. He didn't know if the experience that followed was imagined, or if it had actually happened.

The spirit in front of him began to speak. "Michael, long ago you were marked by destiny. I chose you and nurtured you until this moment. Do you know that this is true?" the being inquired.

"I know it is true," Michael responded. "I have known it since I was a boy."

"The time is drawing near when your destiny will be fulfilled. Even though you have been given outstanding gifts, you will not be able to bear this great responsibility without my assistance. I am willing to help you, but I must be able to depend on your complete obedience.

"The kingdoms of this world are mine, and I give them to whomsoever I choose. Michael Arachev, I have chosen you. Will you accept this destiny by bowing before me in worship and obedience?"

Michael's answer came slowly but surely, "I will." He dropped to his knees there on the pinnacle of the Temple Mount. As he bowed his head to the ground before the being in front of him, he felt a surge of energy flow through him.

The being spoke again, "Michael Arachev, because you have accepted this challenge, I now anoint you Child of Destiny, Son of Perdition. And you shall reign over all the earth!"

Arachev lifted his head just in time to see the being vanish. The last thing he saw was the flash of a gold pentagram around its neck. At that moment, he knew it was Lucifer.

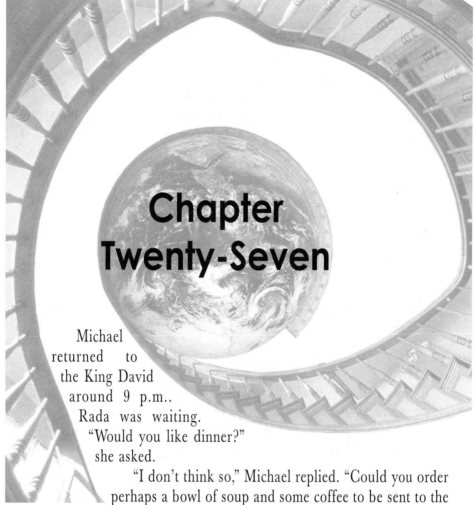

Chapter
Twenty-Seven

Michael returned to the King David around 9 p.m.. Rada was waiting. "Would you like dinner?" she asked.

"I don't think so," Michael replied. "Could you order perhaps a bowl of soup and some coffee to be sent to the room? That's all I want. Order whatever you want for yourself."

While waiting for their food to be delivered, Michael sat quietly in the corner of the room. In his mind, he was replaying the evening's experience, trying to recapture every moment. He was a man of vision, but he had never experienced anything as clearly as what he had experienced on the Temple Mount. He was certain he would do what Jesus had failed to do. He could hear the words as distinctly as when they were first spoken, "I now anoint you...Child of Destiny...Son of Perdition." And then, the flash of the pentagram.

"Did you enjoy your visit to the Temple Mount?" Rada asked. She sensed something extraordinary was going on within Michael. She wanted to know what had happened, if he was willing to talk about it.

"There is something about that place that I don't fully understand," Michael replied. "I don't think there is another place on earth quite like it." That's as far as Michael would go. He shared almost everything with Rada–but not this. The encounter was too personal... too intimate.

Foreign Minister Dore picked them up the next morning at their usual time of 8 a.m. "Good morning, Rada, Michael." They had been together enough so that they now spoke to each other on a first-name basis. "Michael, did you enjoy your time at the Temple Mount last night?"

"I did, Josef," came Michael's reply. "It's quite an unusual place."

"Did you know that there have been more wars fought over the Temple Mount than over any other place on the planet?" Josef inquired. "It seems as though all the great world leaders can't leave it alone. Even if they control the world, they seem compelled to try to lay claim to this site."

"Why is that?" Rada asked.

"I don't know," Josef responded. "The religious Jews say it is because Jerusalem is the place where God chose to place His name. It says that thirty-seven times in the Old Testament. The rabbis teach that the temporal rulers become seized with a compulsion to rule that which God has said only He would rule."

"That's so interesting!" Rada exclaimed. "I wonder if there is anything to it."

Their schedule called for them to be in Tiberius in northern Israel by evening. They took the route through the West Bank, by Jericho, and up through the fertile Jordan Valley.

As they moved through the West Bank, Foreign Minister Dore explained that this was the area known as the occupied territories. "It is also the biblical area known as Judea," he added.

"So this is part of the Promised Land as described in the Bible?" Rada asked.

"Yes," Dore answered. "The biblical boundaries of the Promised Land extended from the River of Egypt in the south to Lebanon in the north; from the Mediterranean in the west to the Euphrates River in the northeast. The promised area even extended into part of what is now Jordan."

"So who lives here now?" Michael asked.

Dore explained, "The Romans drove most of the Jews out of this area in seventy A.D. when they conquered Jerusalem, destroying our Second Temple. After almost two thousand years of Jewish exile, the UN partitioned the land between Jews and Arabs in 1947. This resulted in an Arab-initiated war.

"For the next nineteen years after that war, Jordan controlled the West Bank area, the territory between Jerusalem and the Jordan River. However, never having laid claim to the land, Jordan never annexed it, so it remained disputed territory during this time.

"Then came the 1967 War, during which Israel conquered the land all the way to the Jordan River. Today, approximately two hundred-thousand Jews live there in what is called 'the settlements.' 1.6 million Palestinians live there also. Ownership of this area is one of the most difficult disputes we have. The Jews know it is part of their Promised Land, and yet the Arabs feel that the Jews are intruders here."

As they moved northward through the Jordan Valley, Michael turned to Dore. "What do the Jews believe concerning their Messiah?"

"Most Jews believe that a man, an anointed man, will come someday to bring peace to Israel. Secular Jews pay little attention to it. They contend that we must live our lives for today. However, the religious Jews in Israel believe we are now living in the messianic age. They believe that the rebirth of the nation of Israel indicates this, and regard the appearance of the Messiah as imminent."

"What do most Jews think the Messiah will do when he comes?" Arachev probed. Rada looked at him inquisitively. He was certainly showing more interest in this than normal. She wondered silently if this had anything to do with his visit to the Temple Mount the previous evening. He had been markedly different ever since his return.

"It basically boils down to this," Dore explained. "When Messiah comes, he will do two things: He will bring peace and security to Israel, and He will rebuild our temple."

"Interesting," Arachev said thoughtfully.

As they entered the outskirts of Tiberius, Michael and Rada caught their first view of the Sea of Galilee.

Michael drank in every detail of the geography. Knowing that he was coming to Israel, he had taken time to read the gospel of Luke, which tells of the life of Jesus. Though he did not believe the biblical teachings about Jesus, he found himself in awe of the territory about which most of the gospels were written. He wondered what Jesus was like when He walked in this area nearly 2,000 years before.

Despite these thoughts, Michael reminded himself that his mission would ultimately supercede that of Jesus. "Where Jesus failed to establish a world government, I will succeed," he thought to himself. "He failed to bring peace to the earth, but I will soon outlaw war forever."

Before retiring for the evening, Michael and Rada sat on the balcony of their hotel room overlooking the Sea of Galilee. Turning to Rada, Michael mused, "And to think this was the headquarters of the simple carpenter who influenced the world more than any other human being."

Rada smiled as she replied, "You have to admit that it's more than a little awe-inspiring. Michael, do you think Jesus walked on water as the Bible records?"

"Oh, come now, Rada," Michael replied. "You don't think that event happened do you? The myth of this place must be getting to you, my dear."

Rada laughed self-consciously. "Of course, you are right. It was a foolish question."

Michael wanted to talk. "Rada, we need to realize that our mission is more important than that of Jesus. Just think. Jesus failed in His efforts to bring peace on earth, but we will succeed. Jesus was never able to unify mankind, but that is our destiny." Rada had never heard Michael speak with such conviction. She could tell that he believed every word he was saying, and she believed in him.

Rada lovingly leaned over and kissed him on the cheek. "Let's go to bed, Michael," she said. "It's been a long day."

Chapter Twenty-Eight

The peace award ceremony was scheduled for 8 a.m. the next morning. It was to be held in a beautiful area along the shores of the Sea of Galilee. Foreign Minister Dore was there, along with the mayor of Tiberius and other dignitaries. Michael's good friend, Simon Pervis had traveled all the way from Jerusalem to be a part of the festivities.

Miriam Edelstein of the Peace Institute presented the award. "Mr. Arachev, your contribution to the Jewish people and the State of Israel has been outstanding. For many years, Jewish people in the Soviet Union had longed to make their way to Eretz Israel, but they had been hindered by governmental regulations. Under your presidency, the restrictions were lifted, allowing the yearnings of many years to be realized. Some 650,000 individuals were able to finally 'come home' because of your assistance. For this, the Jewish people owe you a tremendous debt of gratitude. On behalf of these individuals and the entire nation of

Israel, I am honored to present to you Israel's highest peace prize, the Peace Institute Award."

Upon presenting the award, 25 doves were released into the air. One of them hovered near Arachev, finally landing squarely on his head. Arachev stood still. The crowd applauded wildly.

As the people began to disperse, Miriam Edelstein came to tell the Arachevs goodbye. "What a wonderful ceremony!" she exclaimed. "Do you realize that in all the years we have been presenting this award, we have never had one of the doves land on the head of the award winner? I think it was an omen. You are truly a man of peace."

In that moment, Rada's eyes locked with Michael's. They smiled at each other knowingly, both of them thinking: "If she only knew."

Their flight back to the United States was scheduled to leave that evening. As the limousine sped toward Tel Aviv, Arachev was deep in thought, mentally reviewing his experiences in the land of Israel.

As they traveled, it became crystal clear to Michael that the Middle East was the focal point of the clash between two intractable world forces—Islam and Judeo-Christian beliefs.

"That's it!" Michael thought to himself. "Peace is impossible as long as both forces claim exclusive possession of truth. The key to peace is to teach the human race to show tolerance and respect for all religious beliefs." Michael glowed with inner satisfaction, realizing that he now understood the cornerstone to peace on earth and the coming New World Order.

On the plane ride home, Michael discussed his conclusions with Rada. "There simply cannot be peace when people claim to possess the truth to the exclusion of all others," Michael expounded. "It is the formula for unending conflict. That's what we witnessed between Israel and the Muslims."

"So what we suspected back in college has proven to be true," Rada observed. "When Politburo member Gorky said that religious conflict was the source of all war, he was right!"

Michael stated with total conviction, "Ultimately, we will have to outlaw religious exclusiveness. It must become the most hateful and poisonous crime of all."

"Do you have any ideas as to how that can be accomplished?" Rada asked.

"Actually I do," Michael replied quickly. "The Genocide Treaty outlaws doing harm to minorities or groups, whether they are racial, religious or sexual. It not only outlaws physical harm, but it also prohibits causing mental harm, such as the deep hatred that exists in both Palestinian and Israeli children. It must be outlawed."

"Michael, does that include controlling what parents teach their children?" Rada asked with a certain amount of skepticism.

"It's the only way!" Michael declared vehemently. "Until this world adopts proper thinking, and until we establish a culture of peace, wars will continue."

Rada began to understand Michael's intentions.

Chapter Twenty-Nine

After returning to the United States, the Arachevs continued to network with the key players contributing to the advancement of globalization. The ratification process for the World Court was progressing smoothly, in spite of the President's decision to withdraw the United States' signature from the treaty. The Millennium Declaration was becoming well accepted around the world. Interfaithism was rapidly becoming the 'in crowd's' spiritual philosophy. "Yes, everything is moving in the right direction," Michael thought to himself, "but much too slowly."

On the morning of September 11, 2001, Arachev turned on his television for the news. The first thing he saw was a 747 jet plunging into one of the towers of the World Trade Center in New York. "Oh, no!" Arachev exclaimed. Rada came running. Seventeen minutes later, the other tower was hit.

"What's happening, Michael?" Rada asked.

"I don't know, but I can guess. It's the Muslims," Michael said matter-of-factly.

"How can you be sure?" Rada questioned.

Michael answered, "I've been expecting this for a long time. It was inevitable. When two forces are intent on dominating the world, something has to give. If neither of them is willing to back down, then sooner or later it will result in armed conflict."

Over the next few months, Arachev watched with interest as the U.S. moved against Afghanistan and then Iraq. It was obvious from the President's own words that he was determined to take down all who opposed the United States and its War on Terrorism.

In the meantime, the fear generated by 9/11 was enabling governments around the world to intrude into the privacy of individual lives as never before. National ID cards were being adopted, worldwide databases were being set up, and cameras were installed in public places so that an individual's every move could be recorded. Over two million cameras were installed in London alone! Michael understood that, when the time came, these developments would make it that much easier to enforce compliance to his New World Order.

It soon became obvious that America had decided to establish a new world order in its own image. The U.S. had the economic and military dominance to move unilaterally without consulting the world community, and proceeded to do just that.

Arachev knew that the present course of events could not continue for long. Most world leaders understood how close they were to establishing the dream of a one-world socialist society. The Marxist dream had been instilled in each of them since their youth. They weren't about to let the United States sweep away nearly 100 years of work and careful planning without putting up a fight. Michael's intelligence sources were telling him that anti-American sentiment was growing stronger around the world. The big question was, "When would the final showdown occur?"

It wasn't likely to be over Iraq. Not even over Iran. But North Korea? That was another matter. If the United States moved against North Korea, would China stand aside?

World observers had projected that the 21st century would belong to the Chinese. China, with its galloping economy, would pass the U.S. in gross national product by 2015. China was using the economic surpluses generated by a booming economy to rapidly modernize its military forces. Would China stand with North Korea in an American conflict, as was the case during the Korean War of the early 1950s? Or would China choose to face the U.S. alone, later?

Michael sat alone in his study for hours, mulling over the possible scenarios. He didn't see how China could remain aloof in the case of a Korean-American conflict, yet going to war against America might be akin to committing national suicide.

Arachev's intelligence sources informed him that China was devoting huge resources to preparing for cyber warfare. If America's technological advantage could be negated by disabling her advanced weaponry, then 280 million Americans would be pitted against 1.3 billion Chinese. The advantage would suddenly shift to China. Before Arachev could solidify his conclusions, world events suddenly lurched out of control.

Word came to U.S. intelligence that North Korea was two months away from actually producing its first nuclear bomb. The United States had made it clear it would not tolerate a nuclear-armed North Korea.

Two aircraft carriers were already in the region. Three more were given orders to proceed in that direction with all speed. The U.S. announced that it would blockade North Korea, demanding the immediate dismantling of the nuclear facility under international supervision.

North Korea responded with a threat of its own. "The American blockade is a violation of our national sovereignty. We already have several nuclear weapons and the missile capability of delivering them. Any ship moving to impede our Korean vessels will be sunk."

The next day the United States attempted to board a North Korean freightliner. The freightliner resisted, attempting to run the blockade. The American warship fired warning shots across the freightliner's bow. North Korean fighter planes suddenly appeared out of nowhere to strafe the American ship. The American vessel returned fire, downing two of the Korean planes. Then the bombs began to fall. Within one hour, the American ship listed badly to the side and slipped beneath the waters of the South Pacific.

At 4 a.m. the next morning, the U.S. launched a devastating strike upon North Korea's suspected nuclear facility. By 10 a.m., the one million North Korean troops stationed along the demilitarized zone had launched a full-scale invasion of the South. Since the U.S. had withdrawn its 37,000 troops from the DMZ the previous year, South Korea was left to face the massive onslaught alone. With the South Korean capital of Seoul only 36 miles away, the result was inevitable. In two days, the government of South Korea was forced to flee into exile.

An emergency session of the UN Security Council was convened. China called for a temporary ceasefire so the combatants could back away from the precipice of all-out war, but the U.S. would settle for nothing less than the total withdrawal of North Korean troops from the South. The United States' position as the leader of the world was at stake. The U.S. knew it, and so did China.

The next day, the United States launched blistering bombing raids against the military establishments of North Korea. These were largely ineffective since North Korea had evacuated the areas just as soon as hostilities had broken out. The U.S. was faced with the quandary of how to attack the North Korean forces now in South Korea. If the U.S. used its superior air power, It would have to bomb South Korean territory. This would undoubtedly result in large numbers of South Korean civilian casualties.

In Afghanistan and Iraq, the U.S. military had become accustomed to an enemy that reacted to its military initiatives. Now, all of a sudden, America was being forced to deal with an enemy that was seizing the initiative.

The atmosphere was tense as the top military strategists filed into the Oval Office. The President wasted no time with niceties. "All right everyone, where do we stand, and what do you recommend?" he inquired abruptly.

Defense Secretary George Rockford began, "Mr. President, our situation is difficult. By quickly taking control of South Korea, the North has greatly reduced our available options. If we bomb their troops, we will slaughter large numbers of South Korean civilians. Attempting to take out North Korea's leadership has very little chance of success. Osama bin Laden and Saddam Hussein taught us how elusive a well-funded, well-protected leader can be. It will take months to build up an adequate force in the region for a ground invasion. In the meantime, North Korea is solidifying its hold on the South."

"George, what are your recommendations?" the President cut in.

"Mr. President, as my advisors and I see it, we have three choices: we can appeal to the UN to force North Korea's withdrawal from the South; we can maintain the status quo for the next five months while we move five-hundred thousand troops into the region; or we can carpet bomb the DMZ, clearing out a path for the fifty thousand troops that we do have in the area to move in. This would enable us to split North Korea's forces in two, hopefully forcing a surrender of those troops in the South. We could then continue to use our superior air power to protect our troops. This would give us a base on the ground until more troops could be rushed to the area."

The President thought for a moment and then spoke, "Appealing to the UN is out. The world is laughing at us because of the situation we're in. They've been waiting for us to fail ever since we bypassed them on the Iraq crisis.

"As ruthless as the North Korean government is, if we wait five months to liberate South Korea, there will be nothing left to save. Every person upon whom we could rebuild the government would be slaughtered.

"It appears that choice number three is feasible, and could give the enemy something to think about for a while. Let's do it, ladies and gentlemen!"

One week later, the bombing campaign against North Korea began. The main bases used for the operation were the two aircraft carriers in the region and the American military bases in nearby Japan.

The first night of bombing could only be described as horrendous! The "shock and awe" that was promised to Iraq, but never delivered, was executed in full measure against the North Koreans. As he observed the operations, U.S. Defense Secretary Rockford thought, "That will get their attention."

A few minutes later, an urgent message arrived at the U.S. command center for the Asian Pacific that made Rockford take notice. "Mr. Secretary, there has been a powerful missile attack on our bases in Japan. Most of our planes have been destroyed. The devastation is so great that we suspect the bomb had to be nuclear."

One hour later, another extremely disturbing report came to the Secretary: "When our planes attempted to land on their home-base aircraft carriers upon returning from their bombing missions against North Korea, they came under heavy air attack from North Korean planes. The attackers were successfully repulsed and normal landing operations were resumed. Then our big trouble began.

"When the USS Kitty Hawk left the Straits of Taiwan three weeks ago to lend her assistance in the waters off of North Korea, the two Chinese Sovremenny aircraft destroyers followed along toward Korea some distance behind. We assumed their purpose was merely to monitor an increasingly volatile situation. However, during the heat of the air battle with the North Koreans, the Chinese ships apparently moved to within firing range of our two carriers. Both of our aircraft carriers sustained direct hits and sank."

Both Rockford and the President knew that China had purchased these aircraft carrier-destroying ships from the Soviets shortly after the U.S. had used its carriers to face them down in the dispute over Taiwan in 1996.

Defense Secretary Rockford reached for the hotline that connected him straight to the President. The answer was immediate, "President Benton here."

"Mr. President—George Rockford. The North Koreans have responded to our first night of bombing by wiping out our military base in Japan, along with the planes stationed there. It appears that the attack was nuclear. With the cooperation of the Chinese, they have also sunk both of our aircraft carriers in the Asian Pacific."

The President broke in, "That's not all, George. The Chinese have launched an invasion against Taiwan."

"May God help us all!" Rockford exclaimed.

The President continued, as cold as steel, "George, you know the contingency plans that we have laid out. There's no time for second-guessing or re-evaluation. Move forward with all speed." The President was immediately escorted by the Secret Service to a predetermined place of safety.

As soon as President Benton arrived at the mobile command headquarters, he picked up the red phone that gave him a direct connection to Beijing. Within seconds, the voice on the other end said, "President Zhiang."

President Benton spoke quickly. "President Zhiang, you've sunk our aircraft carriers, and now you are invading Taiwan. These are grievous acts of war. What is your intention?"

Zhiang's reply was immediate, "President Benton, you have pushed us too far. You are determined to remake the world in the image of America. We are unwilling to allow you to destroy the Marxist vision of world peace. You've gone too far. We must stop you." President Zhiang hung up.

President Benton knew the plan like the back of his hand. For the past 10 years, the United States had understood that China was its number one military threat. The blueprint called for immediately resorting

175

to a nuclear attack. It would be suicidal to attempt a conventional war against a nation of 1.3 billion people.

America's first strike was focused on China's 25 intercontinental missiles and their city-buster nuclear bombs. The hope was that, once these were neutralized, China would listen to reason and suspend hostilities.

President Benton nodded to the ever-present Secret Service agent holding the black box containing the nuclear codes. "Open it," he ordered. Once the nuclear command box was open, the President entered the secret codes. He knew world history was being altered forever.

From China's war room, President Zhiang watched on the radar screen as the American missiles shot from the nuclear-equipped submarines stationed off China's coast. The Chinese would have less than 10 minutes to react. "Did the Americans think we would be foolish enough to leave our nuclear weapons in known locations when we knew this crisis was coming?" Zhiang wondered in amazement. He then turned to his Minister of Defense. "Fire everything we have," he ordered.

The Defense Minister turned pale. "Everything?" he asked incredulously.

"You heard me!" President Zhiang snapped. "Quickly!"

"Yes sir," the Defense Minister responded, regaining his composure. With this, he hurried from the room.

President Benton huddled with Secretary of Defense Rockford in the War Room. Together they watched the radar screens that would give first indication of the success of the strikes against China and show China's response. Almost simultaneously, as the suspected Chinese nuclear locations were hit, 200 missiles were shot from their silos in different locations throughout China.

"What is this?" President Benton shouted. "Are those missiles real or decoys meant to confuse our anti-missile defense system?"

"There's no way to tell, Mr. President," Rockford replied. "We have to try to take them all down." America's anti-missile defense system was still in its infancy. Rockford was sure that it would not be able to cope with this unexpectedly large onslaught.

"George, did we have any idea they had this many missiles? I was told they had around twenty-five."

"Mr. President, that's what our intelligence service conveyed to us," Rockford answered. "Beyond that, we had no idea."

The President nearly spit the next words from his mouth. "I'm starting to wonder who our secret service really works for. First of all, they tell us Saddam Hussein has weapons of mass destruction. We go over Iraq for a year with a fine tooth comb and barely find a few documents in the private home of a scientist investigating the possibility of building a nuclear bomb some day. Now they have told us repeatedly that China possesses twenty-five intercontinental ballistic missiles. War breaks out, and we find ourselves facing at least two hundred that will reach our shores within the next twenty minutes."

"What do you think, George? Can our missile defenses intercept them?" President Benton asked.

Rockford shook his head. "Not a chance, Mr. President," the Secretary replied. "We'll do good to take down half."

"So that means that one-hundred American cities will go up in flames within the next half hour?" President asked, making sure that he understood.

"Either cities or military bases, whichever the Chinese deem as most important," Rockford answered. "That is if these missiles are carrying nukes."

"We have no choice. China has to be eliminated," the President said with finality. "Order Operation Endgame."

"Yes sir," Rockford said with a slight tremor in his voice. Five minutes later, 1,500 missiles shot toward China from their locations across America and around the world.

Chapter Thirty

Indian Prime Minister Meraji had been following developing world events closely. He, too, had known this day would come. And he intended to take advantage of it.

India had put up with continual terrorist attacks from Pakistan for too long. He had wanted to settle the issue once and for all years ago, but pressure from the U.S. prevented him from doing that. America had no right to say anything now. This was his time!

Because India's conventional forces were so superior to Pakistan's, Prime Minister Meraji knew that Pakistan would immediately use nuclear weapons once India's attack was launched. Furthermore, India could lose 500,000 people and still have over 500,000 left. As a matter of fact, a reduction in population would solve many of India's problems. At the same time, Pakistan would be wiped out. Once both Pakistan and China were gone, India would have all the room it needed.

The Prime Minister turned to his computer, typing in the pre-arranged code–"India's Finest Hour." The message was transmitted simultaneously to each critical official and commander. The Indian-Pakistani War was on! And with that, Asia became one blazing nuclear inferno.

Once the war began, it all came down to who could push the buttons the fastest, and who had the most buttons to push.

By this time, America's missiles were arriving on China's mainland. Each missile carried five to ten warheads. Chinese cities were bursting into flames like fireworks on the Fourth of July. Words like "Armageddon" and "Apocalypse" filled the news reports, but none described the total destruction that occurs when temperatures jump instantaneously from 80 degrees to 2,000. A better description was hell on earth!

Fortunately for America, the antimissile defense system worked better than most had imagined. After the system had failed so miserably at stopping the Scud missiles fired at Israel during the 1991 Gulf War, America and Israel had collaborated on improvements. The Arrow II missiles worked much better during Gulf War II. The few failures during that conflict triggered further improvements in the missile design.

All told, only 20 Chinese missiles made it through to their targets. Seven military bases and 13 American cities sustained direct hits by the Chinese attacks. Two million died in Los Angeles. Houston and Chicago were almost totally destroyed. Phoenix, Denver, Atlanta, Charlotte, and Boston were also hit. Twenty million Americans were killed in all, and an equal number were badly wounded.

Chapter Thirty-One

Michael and Rada Arachev were at the home they maintained in Russia, when the war broke out. As they watched the news reports from Korea, China and America, then from India and Pakistan, Rada became increasingly agitated. "This is insanity!" she exclaimed. "Have these leaders lost their minds?"

"This had to happen," Michael said matter-of-factly. "It was inevitable.

"But there are no winners in a horrible conflict like this!" Rada protested.

"I wouldn't be so sure," Michael replied. "I wouldn't be so sure."

"How can you even imply that there could be any benefit when millions–possibly billions are dying in this out-of-control nuclear holocaust?"

"My dear, Rada," Michael replied, "the winners are those who stay out of the war. Don't you see what is happening? China is no more. India and Pakistan will be fourth-rate powers for the next century, and the United States is greatly weakened and will probably turn toward greater isolationism. World leadership will inevitably return to where it historically belongs–Europe.

CNN was the first to call. "Mr. Arachev, would you be our guest on the six o'clock news?"

"Certainly," Arachev responded. "I can be at the studio by five-thirty."

CNN's Moscow correspondent Matt Strong conducted the interview. "Mr. Arachev, can you tell us what you believe, caused this devastating catastrophe?" he began.

"It's very simple, Matt," Arachev explained. "In this day of 'weapons of mass destruction,' nations can no longer act unilaterally. We live in an interdependent world. This is the age of globalization. When nations act on the basis of 'my way or the highway', this is the result."

Strong asked anxiously, "This is the war we all hoped would never happen. Will humankind survive?"

"I believe so," Michael replied thoughtfully. "However, the way our world is governed will be changed forever."

"In what way?" Strong probed.

"We must embrace structures of global governance. The time has come to restructure the UN Security Council, eliminating the veto power that has rendered the UN powerless for too long. We must allow the UN to live up to its full potential."

"Mr. Arachev, has the time come to outlaw nuclear weapons completely?" Strong asked.

"Matt, I had set a goal of a nuclear-free world by 1999," Arachev reminded. "The nations of the world wouldn't cooperate. We can all see the end result. It was the right thing to do then, and it's the right thing to do now. It's unfortunate this terrible conflagration had to happen in order to wake us up."

Strong wanted to hear more of Arachev's plan. "So how would a restructured United Nations have prevented this horrific war?" he asked.

Arachev explained, "One of the categories of crimes under the new International Criminal Court is the Crime of Aggression. This category has been left undefined because nations did not want the necessary power to be placed in the hands of the international community. The Crime of Aggression simply applies to any nation that initiates an armed conflict without UN authorization. The International Court would prosecute any head-of-state who takes military action without UN approval. The vigorous enforcement of this law by the ICC would have prevented this terrible war we have just experienced."

"So, whoever fired the first shot could be placed on trial for initiating this conflict?" Strong probed.

"Absolutely!" Arachev answered vehemently. "And they should! This is a horrendous crime!"

"I couldn't agree with you more, Mr. Arachev," Strong said, nodding vigorously. "Where do we go from here?"

Michael replied without hesitation, "The first thing we must do is create a Global Emergency Commission to deal with the present crisis. It should have unprecedented powers to requisition the equipment needed, to assign contracts to businesses and to utilize the armed forces of different nations without partiality or prejudice. The Commission must have the power to levy a global tax to pay for the mammoth cost of this operation. The commission must have priority access to drugs, medical facilities, and the power to draft medical staff or other personnel needed to do the job."

Strong concluded the newscast, "Mr. Arachev, thank you for shedding light on the world's future path, and thank you for giving us hope. You have done the people of the world a great service this evening."

Later that evening, the phone rang at the Arachev home. It was the Secretary General of the UN.

As soon as Arachev answered, the Secretary spoke. "Michael, I caught your interview on CNN earlier this evening. It was wonderful."

"Thank you very much, Mr. Secretary," Michael replied. "These are terrible times."

The Secretary hurried on, "I've been thinking since the interview. Michael, there are very few leaders with the experience, the vision and the strength of leadership to head a commission like you described on your newscast. I've called to ask you to assume this vital job. As a matter of fact, I insist that you accept. The world needs you at this time. We can count on you, can't we?"

"As you know, Mr. Secretary, this will be a formidable task," Arachev said. "But I don't see how I can turn you down."

"Wonderful, Michael!" the Secretary said enthusiastically. "We want you to start immediately. You'll have the full backing of the entire world community."

Chapter Thirty-Two

It didn't take long for Michael and Rada to prepare the proposals for the inauguration of global governance. They had meticulously worked out the blueprint years ago. They now had the 'go-ahead' for its implementation.

Public opposition was no problem. The hue and cry from every corner was for structures of global government that could deal with unprecedented global problems. Anyone who dared to raise a voice against its emergence was immediately discredited as a nationalist and a warmonger.

Arachev moved fast, as was his trademark. He called for an emergency meeting of the signatories to the International Criminal Court Statute.

The International Court had received the necessary ratifications to take power in April of 2002. This was much quicker than even the globalists had thought possible. Now Arachev wanted to define the Crime of Aggression, which the ICC founding conference in 1998 had left undefined.

The sought-for changes were rushed through with lightning speed. The ICC definition became, 'Crime of Aggression: Any military action taken by a nation without the enactment of a UN resolution authorizing said action.' The UN now had the power of approval or veto over every military action on earth.

The need for a global tax to finance the new world government was so glaringly obvious that opposition to it was futile. The tax would be levied on international flights and international financial transactions. The globalists were beside themselves with glee. Arachev was leading the charge into world government at breakneck speed!

At an emergency meeting of the UN Security Council, the hated and much-maligned 'Big Five' veto power was abolished. The media hailed this as the long overdue move towards a genuine global democracy. Although the U.S. abstained from the vote, it did not use its veto power to block it. With this move, national sovereignty ceased to exist.

The World Health Organization was charged with the daunting task of burying the world's two billion dead, and treating those suffering from nuclear radiation. The pharmaceutical companies producing the drugs used to treat radiation sickness were given huge grants to dramatically increase production.

The sheer size of the emergency forced all of the world's nations to work together to meet the unprecedented challenge. This accelerated the unification of the world into a one-world body. The United Nations now commandeered activities that previously would have been handled by sovereign states. The world government train had left the station, and nothing was going to stop it.

Michael Arachev's new job as head of Global Security kept his name and face in the headlines on a daily basis. He seemed to be everywhere and to have the answers before most of the world's leaders had thought of the questions. It was obvious to everyone that he was a man made for the job!

The catastrophe thrust upon the world was so vast and the transition into world government so swift, that people could barely remember how things were before World War III. It was similar to the sea of change that took place after 9/11, only magnified a thousand times. Simply stated, the transformation was nothing short of total revolution.

Chapter Thirty-Three

In his weekly meeting with the Secretary General, Arachev made his next move. "Mr. Secretary, as head of Global Security, I would be negligent in my job if I did not move aggressively to solve the one situation that could once again threaten world peace. We must solve the Israeli-Palestinian problem, and we must do it before the momentum that we presently enjoy dissipates."

"How would you accomplish this?" the Secretary inquired.

"By facing it directly," Arachev explained. "The world community knows what has to be done, but so far no one has had the courage to do it. No one has wanted to cross the Israelis and the U.S., on the one hand, or the Arab world on the other. The time has come to take the bull by the horns and solve it, once and for all."

"I agree with you, Michael," the Secretary replied. "The situation has been allowed to fester. Do what you must."

"Thank you, Mr. Secretary," Michael said. "We are on our way."

The Secretary General watched with obvious admiration as Michael quickly exited the room. Turning to his executive assistant, he remarked, "Quite a man, that Arachev. I don't think there's another like him in the world."

The assistant nodded in agreement. "I think most of the world is beginning to feel the same way," he remarked.

When Arachev arrived in Israel a week later, he immediately convened meetings with the Israeli and Palestinian Prime Ministers. As was his custom, he plunged straight into the matter at hand. "Gentlemen, I insisted on meeting with you heads-of-state because you have the power to make decisions, not merely talk about making them. I trust that all of us are prepared today to do what we must to ensure world peace."

Both Yigal Alon and Nasser Assam were slightly taken aback by Arachev's whirlwind manner. He was accustomed to this initial response from those who were dealing with him for the first time. He would exploit this to blast them out of their entrenched positions that had prevented progress up to this point.

Palestine's Prime Minister attempted to move the discussion back to familiar ground. "My people are anxious for peace. However, we must regain all territories occupied by Israel, and we must have Jerusalem as our capital. I also have an obligation to defend the downtrodden refugees' right of return to their stolen homes and lands."

Israel's Alon rebutted, "Israelis are desperate for peace, and we are willing to make painful concessions to achieve it. However, I am not willing to risk Israel's security for any reason. We will not be able to return to 1967 borders, since they are indefensible. Furthermore, Jerusalem is the eternal capital of the nation of Israel. It has never been the capital of a Palestinian state, and therefore we will not agree to the re-division of the Holy City."

Arachev clenched his jaws. He looked both leaders squarely in the eyes and in a voice of steel said, "Gentlemen, two billion people have died in the last three months—two billion! The games that past leaders have been playing for the last fifty years are over. I have come here today fully empowered by the UN Secretary General to conclude a final peace agreement for the people of the Middle East. Let's suspend the posturing and get to the heart of the matter.

"Here's what has to be done," Arachev stated emphatically. "Israel must withdraw to pre-1967 borders except for the places where Israeli population concentrations have become dominant. This would consist of about four percent of the West Bank.

"Israelis living in other settlements throughout the occupied territories will be given a choice. They can either relocate, receiving compensation for the homes they leave behind, or they can remain in the territories, living under Palestinian rule."

"Mr. Arachev, that's not a choice," Alon objected. "Israelis will not want to live under a Palestinian government."

"Why not?" Arachev countered. "A million Arabs are living under Israel's rule as Israeli citizens. It's the same thing."

Alon replied with a trace of sarcasm, "Do you think that Palestinians would treat Israelis living under their rule as well as Israel has treated its Arab population?"

Arachev replied, "Everything is changing. Globalization requires new thinking from all of us. Arabs in Israel, Jews in Palestine, Jews in America, Arabs in America. It's a new day, Prime Minister."

Assam broke in, "And what do we get for giving up our historical homelands?"

"You get a sovereign Palestinian state recognized by the international community," Arachev replied. "Throughout Palestinian history, this is something you have never had. You also will be allowed to place your capital in Jerusalem."

Prime Minister Alon vehemently objected. "Jerusalem is our eternal capital. We cannot accept anything else!"

"Mr. Prime Minister, do you want peace or not?" Arachev asked impatiently. "You know that this issue is a deal-breaker. Jerusalem will be your capital as well. It will remain undivided."

"How do you expect to accomplish that feat?" Alon inquired.

"Sometimes we have to change our way of thinking in order to reach solutions. The Old City will be shared, and will not be under any nation's sovereignty."

"Who will govern it?" Alon asked.

Arachev explained, "The Secretary General will serve as the Mayor of Jerusalem. An Arab Deputy Mayor will administer the areas populated by Arabs, and a Jewish Deputy Mayor will administer areas where Jews live."

Arachev could feel the Israeli Prime Minister's resolve hardening against his proposals. His instincts told him it was time to sweeten the deal. He continued, "The Temple Mount will be shared as well."

"You know that is totally unacceptable to us, Mr. Arachev," Assam protested. "The entirety of the Haram al Sharif is a Muslim mosque and must remain so."

"Prime Minister Assam," Arachev warned, "It is not possible for everyone to have everything they want. Without compromise, there can be no peace. Those who attempt to gain everything will ultimately lose everything."

"What do you mean by sharing?" Prime Minister Alon inquired.

"Muslims will worship at Muslim holy sites, and Jews will worship at Jewish holy sites," Arachev stated. "You could even build your Third Temple there." When Arachev mentioned the possibility of building the temple, it was as though someone had sucked the air from the room.

"This will not work," Assam stated vehemently. "It's intolerable!"

"It will work," Arachev countered without blinking an eye. "There's no reason why it won't."

"But you're asking us to give up everything," Assam protested.

Arachev reviewed the proposal. "You're receiving a Palestinian state, a homeland with internationally recognized borders, and your capital in Jerusalem. Israel gives up her ancestral homeland of Judea-Samaria and surrenders sovereignty over her eternal capital of Jerusalem."

"We won't do it," Assam stated adamantly.

Arachev decided to make his final offer. "Prime Minister, peace is within our grasp. If you miss this opportunity, the world community will wash its hands of the Middle East. You and Israel can continue killing each other. All international economic aid will stop, and the UN will not come to the aid of the Palestinian cause anymore, even if Israel decides that Palestinians are to be totally banished from the Promised Land."

The Palestinian Prime Minister knew when he was defeated. He reached for the pen to sign the agreement that Arachev pushed across the table toward him.

As the Israeli Prime Minister signed, Arachev was sure that he saw a reflection of the Third Temple glimmering in his eyes.

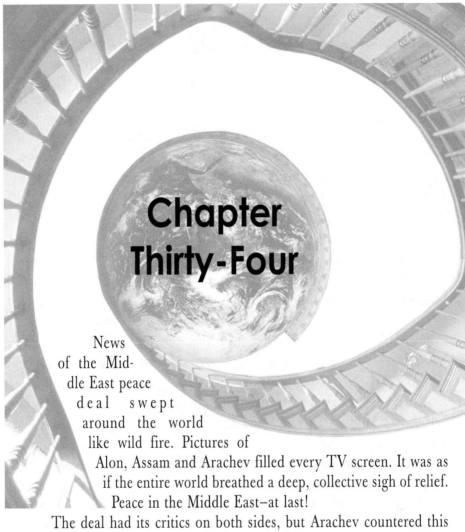

Chapter Thirty-Four

News of the Middle East peace deal swept around the world like wild fire. Pictures of Alon, Assam and Arachev filled every TV screen. It was as if the entire world breathed a deep, collective sigh of relief. Peace in the Middle East—at last!

The deal had its critics on both sides, but Arachev countered this by appearing on every major talk show to tout the benefits of the agreement. The average Palestinian and Israeli felt hopeful for the first time in decades.

Palestinians finally had their state—a place to call home. Israelis were tempted to dream of entering the messianic era as plans were being drawn for the building of their Third Temple—the first temple in 2,000 years. Tourism to Israel and Palestine was running at record levels. In addition, the world economy was booming as major industries were rapidly recovering from the devastation inflicted by the war.

The expiration of the UN Secretary General's term was only three months away. As usual, the rumor mills were buzzing with the names of possible successors. However, it was quickly becoming apparent that a consensus existed on who should be elected for the job. Hands down, it had to be Michael Arachev. He was the man with the vision. He was the man with the answers. The world needed him.

By the time the UN Security Council met to elect the new Secretary General, the process was a mere formality. Because France held the Council presidency, its UN ambassador called the meeting to order. "Ladies and gentlemen, our meeting today is of the highest importance. We are here to elect the next leader of the United Nations.

"I want to thank our outgoing Secretary General Mugavo for his outstanding service. He has presided over the shaping of global governance during the most difficult of times. His dignity and grace through humankind's greatest disaster has helped to ensure the world's survival." Turning to Mugavo, he said, "Mr. Secretary General, we thank you for your faithful service." The entire Security Council rose to its feet in a standing ovation. The Secretary General stood, and with a nod, acknowledged the applause.

The French ambassador continued, "And now ladies and gentlemen, the chair will consider nominations for the post of Secretary General."

The ambassador from Russia rose to his feet. "Mr. Chairman," he began, "It is with great pleasure that the Russian Federation nominates for the office of Secretary General a man who hails from Russia and has shown himself to be a world-class leader. Russia nominates Mr. Michael Arachev."

"Thank you, Mr. Ambassador," the French ambassador responded. "Are there other nominations for the office of Secretary General?" Each ambassador looked expectantly around the room at his fellow ambassadors. No one made a move.

After waiting a respectable amount of time, the chairman proceeded. "We have only one nomination for the office of Secretary General of the United Nations," he said. "We will now proceed with the vote."

After the votes were tallied, the French ambassador announced the results, "Ladies and gentlemen, we have a new UN Secretary General by unanimous election–Mr. Michael Arachev." The council members applauded enthusiastically. The Council President continued, "Knowing the prevailing sentiment of this Council, I requested that Mr. Arachev be here at UN headquarters today. I thought it would be fitting if he were present to accept this position in person." About that time, the Council President's aides ushered Michael and Rada into the Security Council chambers. Thunderous applause broke out across the room.

The French ambassador continued, "Today, we are entering a new era. When our last Secretary General was elected, the United Nations was weak and in disarray. That has changed. Through our recent catastrophe, the world has discovered that there is no substitute for effective international law. Strong global government requires strong leadership. You have just elected a man proven to be an outstanding leader. In my opinion and yours, he is the finest leader in the world today. It is now my distinct honor to present to this Council our new Secretary General and leader of the world, Mr. Michael Arachev." The council members broke into loud and sustained applause as Arachev moved toward the podium.

As the applause continued, Arachev stood at the podium, savoring the moment. Flashing through his mind were those times when he realized destiny was upon him. His thoughts turned to the night when the Germans had captured his grandfather. He recalled how clear it was to him on that occasion that world government and the unity of all humankind was the only road to peace on earth. He remembered the more recent encounter on the Temple Mount. He realized his life-long destiny had become reality. He, Michael Arachev, was now the undisputed leader of the world!

Finally, he held up his hands for silence. "Thank you. Thank you very much," he said. "It is with full realization of the great responsibility you have placed on me that I accept the challenge to work with you to lead the world into a new order of peace and security. We have had enough war! We have had enough of conflict! We must relegate to the past those things leading to hatred and strife.

"Ladies and gentlemen, destiny calls. We must allow nothing to stop us. War must be outlawed. National rivalries and religious strife must be banished forever. We will do it. We have the strength, and we have the resolve. And we will not rest until the human race is at rest. Join with me. Together we will not fail. United, we will succeed."

As Arachev returned to his seat beside Rada, the applause was deafening.

Chapter Thirty-Five

Michael Arachev moved quickly to consolidate his power. With China destroyed, world leadership swiftly shifted to Europe. While the United States moved toward an increasingly isolationist stance in world affairs, Russia continued to pursue an integrationist policy with the European Union. The vision of a 'common European home' from the Atlantic Ocean to the Ural Mountains became a reality.

In the meantime, UN peacekeeping forces assumed their responsibilities in the Middle East. The blue-helmeted soldiers were now a common sight in Jerusalem. They were especially visible on the Temple Mount itself.

The United Nations moved swiftly to grant full membership in the world body to the new Palestinian State. Israel proceeded with her withdrawals from most of the Judean settlements. Arachev was quite surprised at how many of the settlers decided to remain there under

Palestinian rule. They were a brave and stubborn lot, and their convictions were apparently more genuine than he had thought. In his mind, Arachev felt sure that those who stayed would live to someday regret their decision. Nevertheless, the historic agreement was being implemented.

The news that captured world attention was the building of Israel's Third Temple. The Israelis moved faster than Arachev had believed possible. Most of the world did not realize it, but religious leaders in Israel had already prepared architectural drawings for the building of the temple. When Israel began preparing the area north of the Dome of the Rock for the start of construction, minor skirmishes broke out. However, the UN troops did as they had been ordered. They put down the uprisings ruthlessly. They had been instructed to tolerate no resistance, and they followed orders to the letter.

When the walls of the temple were raised, the event occupied the news around the world for many days. Even Michael did not understand the fascination associated with the Temple Mount. WNN and other news services featured daily updates concerning the temple's construction.

Speculation was rife. Would the construction of Israel's temple trigger the appearance of the Messiah, as many religious Jews believed? America's Evangelical Christians were adamant that the construction of the temple was a certain sign that the Second Coming of Christ was imminent.

The temple's construction produced an incredible resurgence in Christianity, catching Arachev and most world leaders by surprise. People who had not attended church for years suddenly recommitted their lives to Jesus Christ. Church and ministry incomes rose dramatically. As a result, churches' evangelistic efforts became aggressive and far-reaching. Radio, television, the Internet and print media were literally abuzz with talk of the temple being rebuilt and its significance in the fulfillment of Bible prophecy.

Churches that had only 200 in attendance suddenly jumped to 500 and then to 1,000. Classes explaining the prophecies of the Bible were increasingly in demand. Prophecy conferences that previously had 500 in attendance had 5,000. These conferences fueled the surging church growth. For the first time in 100 years, the world began experiencing a true religious revival. Most alarming to the globalists was the rate at which this religious renaissance was accelerating around the world. The Internet allowed movements to become global almost instantaneously.

Christianity wasn't the only religion to experience revival. In Israel, 'Messiah fever' was raging. The building of the first temple in 2,000 years struck a chord deep within the Jewish soul. Rabbis were proclaiming that the temple was a prophetic fulfillment straight from Scripture. And, of course, many false messiahs appeared around the Western Wall and on the Temple Mount itself.

The ranks of young rabbis-in-training swelled dramatically. Jerusalem's Temple Institute worked diligently to train the young priests in order for them to minister in the new temple when it was completed.

Most interesting of all was the debate that raged over the Messiah. Would He immediately appear? Was He in their midst already? How would they know Him when He did show up? The Jews as a whole believed that Messiah would do two things when He came. He would bring peace and security to Israel, and He would build their temple. It appeared that the Jewish nation was experiencing both of those things. Could Messiah's appearance be far behind?

Chapter Thirty-Six

The insiders met for their annual meeting at the Presidio in San Francisco with mixed emotions. They had never been nearer to their goal of world government, yet the worldwide religious resurgence was making them nervous.

Morris Samuels opened the meeting. "As all of you know, we live in a different world than we did a year ago," he began. "Last year, we had a population of six billion. This year we suddenly have four billion. Last year, there was still significant resistance to world government. This year, it is being embraced as the only answer to the challenges that we face. The failure of the old world order has accelerated our progress into the new one. However, the price for this global awakening has been terrible."

Samuels continued, "The goals that this group has worked toward for many years are now being realized. The fact that the world turned to one of our members for leadership in its greatest hour of crisis is the ultimate validation. The world is now discovering what we have known for many years—that Michael Arachev is the greatest leader the world has ever seen." With that statement, the room broke into applause.

"One more thing before I conclude my opening remarks," Morris stated. "It would be a mistake for us to relax because we appear to have won the battle for the future of the world. It's possible to win the war and lose the peace. I'm simply saying that our work is not over, by any means."

"You know Morris," Theodore Joiner spoke up, "I'm as excited by the rapid advances into globalization as anybody. But I will admit that I'm quite disturbed by this sudden religious surge that's been produced by the building of the Jews' temple.

"I know what religion is all about. I was raised in a religious home. When a religious wave sweeps through a society, it can overwhelm every force that gets in its way. We're facing a problem that can't be ignored."

Arachev had anticipated the direction that this year's meeting would take. "Theodore, I must agree," Michael began. "I believe that religious radicals are the most lethal threat we face. For this reason, I invited Rabbi Isaacs from the Jewish community and Cardinal Agnola Calogera, Secretary of State for the Vatican to be in our meeting today. They are presently standing by in the lounge. If all of you are agreeable, I'd like for them to participate in this discussion."

Bishop Hanscom of the United Religions spoke up. "Bring them in."

Arachev's executive assistant ushered Rabbi Isaacs and Cardinal Calogera into the room. After introductions, Michael moved right to the point. "Both of you believe in and support the New World Order. There is one remaining threat that could jeopardize the achievements of those who truly value world peace. I refer to the religious fervor that has recently swept across Israel and the United States, and has started to affect the rest of the world. We're hoping that you can explain to us the forces behind this sudden religious resurgence."

Rabbi Isaacs moved to the edge of his chair as he began to speak, "I cannot address what is happening from the Christian perspective, but I can speak for the nation of Israel. The belief that someday Messiah will come is deeply ingrained in the soul of the Jewish nation. Even those

Jews who claim to not believe in God somehow still harbor the possibility that they may be wrong, and that Messiah will come."

The Rabbi continued to explain, "The rebirth of the Jewish nation after two thousand years without a homeland is viewed by most Jews as the beginning of the messianic era. Consequently, Jews have been expecting the appearance of their Messiah since 1948.

"There's one more belief that you must understand. Jews believe that when Messiah comes, he will do two things. He will bring peace and security to Israel, and he will build the Third Temple."

"So it's no wonder that messianic fever is sweeping the nation as a result of the temple being built!" Joiner exclaimed.

"That's right," Rabbi Isaacs agreed, nodding his head.

As the Rabbi spoke, Arachev absorbed every word. The wheels in his head were spinning as he considered the implications of what he was hearing.

The eyes of every person in the room swung to Cardinal Calogera. "Ladies and gentlemen," he began, "the present religious wave in America is beyond anything I have witnessed in my lifetime. It has been a strong belief, among Evangelical Christians in particular, that one of the signs of the Second Coming of Jesus would be the rebuilding of the Jewish temple on the Temple Mount. Frankly, the power of the movement resulting from the Temple's construction has caught the Catholic Church by surprise. Since the Roman Church has not put strong emphasis on the prophecies of the Bible, we did not realize the importance placed on this event among Evangelical Christians.

"But the effect is undeniable. I am being told that financial contributions have quadrupled, and that people are taking early retirement from their jobs and businesses so they can work as volunteer missionaries. This is a movement we must take seriously."

Theodore Joiner turned to Rabbi Isaacs. "So Jews believe that whoever brings peace and security to Israel and builds their temple is the Messiah?" he asked.

"Yes," the Rabbi replied.

Joiner pressed the issue, "Has it dawned on them yet that Michael Arachev has brought peace to Israel and made the building of the temple possible?" At this, eyebrows around the room were raised.

Rabbi Isaacs responded, "It may surprise you, but just last week there was an article published in Israel presenting that very possibility."

"Are you saying that an article was written questioning whether Arachev is the Messiah?" Joiner asked in astonishment.

"Yes. Absolutely," Isaacs answered.

Morris Samuels had been watching the expression on Michael's face during this exchange. Arachev was following the conversation with extreme interest, but he didn't act the slightest bit surprised. Morris thought to himself, "Is there a chance that Michael sees himself as the Messiah?"

Cardinal Calogera chimed in, "The Pope believed Mr. Arachev would be the best possible leader to head the New World Order. He fully supported Mr. Arachev's election to UN Secretary General."

"I have an idea," Joiner said abruptly. "I think I know how to stop this religious frenzy. We'll fight fire with fire by starting our own religious movement in order to counteract the one threatening our New World Order," Joiner explained. "We can actually turn what appears to be a negative into a huge positive for our side."

Arachev knew exactly where this was going, but held his peace, allowing the game to come to him.

Rabbi Isaacs spoke up, "You know, this idea may not be as preposterous as it seems. Our sages tell us that a potential messiah is born in every generation. However, we are taught that no one has ever become the Messiah because the world has not yet been prepared to receive him. I have to say that, if there is a potential messiah in this generation, it has to be Michael Arachev. Furthermore, I have never known of a time in all of history when the world was as ready to receive its Messiah as it is now."

Understanding the tremendous level of influence exercised by the Vatican on the world, Samuels turned to Cardinal Calogera. "How would Pope Peter II view what we are discussing today?" he asked.

Everyone knew that the answer to this question was key. Without the support of the Pope, who now represented one-fourth of the world's inhabitants, the whole idea was doomed.

Cardinal Calogera's answer surprised everyone. "As was his predecessor, Pope Peter is a fierce advocate of one-world government. He believes that the United Nations is a divinely-ordained authority for global governance. Also, he is a long-time friend and admirer of Mr. Arachev. Since its inception, the Roman Church has made political-religious alliances with the ruling authorities of the day."

Samuels sensed this was a possibility that should be explored further. "Cardinal Calogera," he asked, "do you think the Pope would find an alliance between Michael Arachev and himself desirable?"

Those in the room could almost see the Cardinal's mind weighing carefully what he should say. Finally, he spoke, "Actually, the Pope and I have discussed this possibility. If Mr. Arachev would be willing to acknowledge the Pope as the supreme spiritual leader on earth, I believe His Holiness is prepared to proclaim him the political leader of the world."

Never one to let a good opportunity pass when he saw one, Theodore Joiner asked immediately, "How should we form this alliance?"

"Mr. Arachev will need to visit the Vatican. There, as he bows to acknowledge the spiritual supremacy of the Pope, His Holiness will pronounce Mr. Arachev, Emperor of the Holy Roman Empire and of the New World Order. This will elevate Mr. Arachev to a level never before bestowed upon a human being."

Morris Samuels carefully watched his friend Michael. Would he agree to this arrangement?

In the meantime, a thought went through Michael's head that he wouldn't share with Morris or anyone else. "I've already bowed to the devil," he mused to himself. "I might as well bow to the Pope."

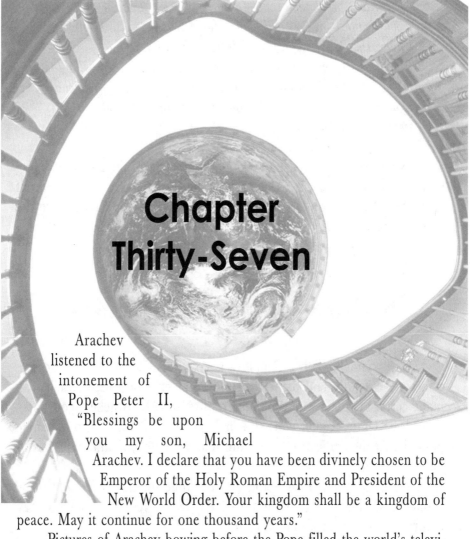

Chapter Thirty-Seven

Arachev listened to the intonement of Pope Peter II, "Blessings be upon you my son, Michael Arachev. I declare that you have been divinely chosen to be Emperor of the Holy Roman Empire and President of the New World Order. Your kingdom shall be a kingdom of peace. May it continue for one thousand years."

Pictures of Arachev bowing before the Pope filled the world's television screens that evening. The establishment press extolled the event as the enthronement of the New World Order—the consummate marriage of politics and religion. Most of the world welcomed the news with open arms.

However, to the evangelical movement, the news was like throwing gasoline onto a fire. Prophecy websites immediately reported on the significance of the event:

"The Bible prophesies that, in the end time, there will be two global leaders—a political leader, the Antichrist, and a religious leader, the False Prophet. Revelation 13 explains that the False Prophet will lend his influence to the Antichrist, causing the world to follow his leadership. This new alliance between Michael Arachev and Pope Peter II appears to be the fulfillment of this important prophecy."

When Arachev's assistant brought a printout of the messages being carried on the prophecy websites to him, Michael was beside himself with rage. "These idiots!" he shouted. "I've given my life to save the world from the scourge of war, and they threaten to wreck everything I have accomplished with their prophetic fantasies!"

When Israel's Third Temple was completed, plans for the dedication were carefully laid. Israel's Prime Minister Alon called Arachev to make certain that he would be able to attend. "Mr. Arachev, you know that all of Israel credits you with making the rebuilding of our temple possible. At the dedication we would like to honor you and express our nation's gratitude."

The date was agreed upon, and the time for the dedication came sooner than Michael thought possible. He arrived in Israel the day before the dedication ceremonies.

As Arachev contemplated the dedication of the Third Temple, he was filled with turmoil. What had he set in motion when he consented to the building of the temple on the Temple Mount? Would tomorrow's ceremonies heighten the religious tidal wave that was already threatening to spin out of control? These thoughts continued, making it difficult for him to sleep.

Somewhere around 2:30 in the morning, Michael finally fell into a restless slumber. Immediately, he found himself engrossed in a turbulent dream. In the dream, there was a war in heaven. Satan and his angels were attempting to overthrow God himself. The struggle was awful! Michael, the archangel, led the armies of heaven in battle. They defeated Satan and his armies, and then banished Satan from heaven, confining him to the earth.

Michael awoke around 4:30 a.m., but it was as though the dream didn't stop. He felt the same presence in the room that he had felt during his experience on the Temple Mount. The presence spoke to him. He wasn't sure whether the voice was audible or simply in his mind, but it was real nonetheless.

"Michael," Satan said, "I've been watching your progress. You've done well in many respects, but the fundamentalist Christians have you bewildered."

Michael responded, "It's true. Everything I do attempting to stop them seems to merely add fuel to the fire."

"In spite of your incredible gifts, Michael," Satan said, "you are discovering that you can't rule this complex world through your own ability. You need me. I will help you, but I need to be in total control. I have come to indwell you this night, Michael Arachev. Will you receive me?"

In Michael's mind, he had no choice. If he was going to stop the Christian tidal wave, he needed Satan's help. Throwing all reservations to the wind, Michael intoned, "I welcome you in, Lucifer. Please come in." At that moment, Michael heard what he could only describe as a swooshing sound, like the wind. Then suddenly he felt energy and an unexplainable self-confidence.

Over breakfast, Arachev read that morning's *Jerusalem Post*. The paper was filled with articles concerning the dedication festivities. An article in the editorial section caught Arachev's attention. It was entitled: "Is Arachev our Messiah?" The article made sense to Michael. "I was born to be the Messiah," he thought to himself, "not to the Jews alone, but to the whole world." With that self-realization, he walked with Rada toward the Mercedes limousine that was waiting outside the King David Hotel.

As the limousine moved through the streets of Jerusalem, Arachev was deep in thought. "So this is what it feels like to be the Messiah, riding through the streets of Jerusalem," he mused to himself. The world didn't yet know who he was, but they would soon enough. As Michael internalized his new sense of identity, he was slightly surprised that he was able to make the adjustment so easily. "Of course, I've had these suspicions for a while," he thought. "So it's not like this is completely new to me."

When they arrived at the appointed meeting place, Michael was impressed by the number of heads-of-state and religious leaders. He saw the presidents of the United States, Russia, Great Britain, France, Italy, Germany, and a host of other countries. In all, 170 out of the 190 nations on earth were represented. Religious leaders included the Archbishop of Canterbury, the head of the United Religions, the Dalai Lama and, of course, Pope Peter II. Arachev had been to many important global events, but he had never seen a meeting quite like this one!

The Temple Mount had been packed to capacity since ten o'clock that morning. People came from everywhere. They filled the Western Wall Plaza. Every roof that commanded a view of the Temple Mount was filled with onlookers. Helicopters hovered overhead, getting as close as Israeli security would allow.

The honored guests were to be the last to enter before the dedication ceremonies began. The most important and final entrants would be Israeli Prime Minister Alon and Israel's Chief Rabbi Cohen, and then Arachev and the Pope. Arachev greeted the Pope as they came together to make their entrance. "Your Holiness," Arachev said, nodding respectfully.

"Michael!" the Pope said warmly. "This is a great day for both of us." The two men understood each other. It was as though they were kindred spirits.

The entrance of the VIPs had already begun. The newly formed Temple Orchestra was playing an inspiring Jewish anthem. The full significance of this occasion engulfed Arachev as he and Rada slowly walked toward their seat of honor in the front row.

As soon as the Arachevs came in view of the crowd, applause began. It became louder and louder, until it totally engulfed the Temple Mount. The intensity of the response might have been embarrassing, but to Michael it was appropriate. He knew who he was, and apparently, the people were starting to understand, too.

When Arachev reached his seat, he turned to get his first look at the new Temple. He had seen the world's most exquisite buildings, but he was not at all prepared for this. The unrivaled beauty and majesty of the Third Temple almost took his breath away.

The Temple was not ostentatious or gaudy. Its lines were simple, but unbelievably elegant. The entire structure was of white marble so pure that it almost appeared to be translucent. Undoubtedly, it was the most beautiful building Michael had ever seen.

The dedication service began with a song of praise by the Temple Choir. Arachev glanced around him. Women were unashamedly weeping as the choir sang. Michael noticed that Prime Minister Alon was tightly clenching his jaw in an attempt to hold back the tears.

Michael analyzed the situation. Here was a people that had been driven from nation to nation over the last 2,000 years. Many, if not most of the Jews present today, had relatives who were killed in Nazi concentration camps. In 1948, their nation was miraculously reborn, and now they were dedicating their temple in their eternal capital of Jerusalem. No wonder they were fighting back tears of joy. No wonder there were those who thought the appearance of the Messiah could not be far away.

When the choir was finished, Prime Minister Alon stepped to the podium. "Secretary General Arachev, His Holiness Pope Peter II, fellow heads-of-state and fellow citizens of the world: On behalf of the citizens of the nation of Israel, I greet you. This is a day like no other in the history of our nation. Jehovah God has gathered us out of the nations where we were scattered because of our sins, and has brought us back to our historic homeland, the land of Israel. For this we are humbled and grateful.

"We thank the United Nations for its vote in 1947 to give birth to this nation. We thank the United States for its undying support, without which we would not have survived. We thank our enemies who have now agreed to live in peace with us so that we can raise our children and our grandchildren together. And I must pause to give proper thanks to the one man, who more than any other, has made it possible for us to dedicate our first temple in 2,000 years, and to worship in peace and security. Thank you Mr. Michael Arachev. Israel owes you an eternal debt of gratitude." With these words, everyone on the Temple Mount rose to their feet, applauding the world's new Secretary General.

Arachev stepped to the speaker's stand waiting for the applause to diminish. Finally he had to raise his arms, motioning for silence. "Thank you. Thank you very much," he began. "We are here today to dedicate a house of worship, not for one people or one religion. As the Scriptures tell us, this Third Temple is to be a house of prayer for all nations. Sectarianism, religious strife and religious exclusiveness have brought mankind nothing but conflict and war. Now the time has come for us to put our divisions behind us forever. We are all brothers and sisters. We are one human race. Let us replace hatred with love; conflict with harmony; hurting with healing; war with peace. If we will do this, the City of Jerusalem will truly become what it was intended to be–the city of peace."

For the third time in less than an hour, the crowd on the Temple Mount broke into thunderous applause for the man who had become a symbol of peace and safety.

While the applause continued to sweep over the Temple Mount, four young rabbis entered onto the Temple Mount Plaza from the western gate. When the people noticed that they were leading a calf, they fell silent. The dignitaries looked at each other questioningly. "Were the rabbis getting ready to make an animal sacrifice?" each person wondered.

It didn't take long for them to get their answer. The rabbis continued straight to the door of the temple's outer court where the brazen altar stood. When they stopped beside the altar, the rabbis quickly threw the calf to the ground, tying its two front legs together and then its two back legs. In one deft movement, they hoisted the calf onto the altar.

The calf began to bawl as it thrashed to get loose. Once it realized its struggle was futile, it lay still.

Chief Rabbi Cohen stepped to the head of the calf and was handed the sacrificial knife by one of the young attendants. Raising the knife into the air, Cohen, with one swift stroke, skillfully severed the animal's jugular vein. The calf jerked its head backwards, convulsing for nearly 15 seconds, and then lay still. Another priest held the vessel designed to catch the blood at the calf's throat. Once the blood was thoroughly drained, the priest carried it into the interior of the temple where it would be sprinkled as atonement for the sins of Israel.

Rabbi Cohen remained at the brazen altar preparing to offer the dedication prayer. "O Lord, God of Abraham, Isaac and Jacob, we know that the heaven of heavens cannot contain You. Yet we have built this house as a place where Your people can meet with You and worship in Your presence. We dedicate this temple to Your glory and to Your praise.

"When King Solomon dedicated the First Temple to You, You signified Your acceptance by sending fire from heaven to consume the sacrifice offered that day. When Elijah conducted the test on Mt. Carmel to determine the true God, You answered his prayer by sending fire upon the sacrifice.

"Lord God, I beseech You this day to show Your acceptance of this house of prayer, and send Your fire so the world may know You are God."

Rabbi Cohen stepped back from the altar in expectation. A hush settled over the Temple Mount crowd. But nothing happened. No one knew what to do next. It was a singularly awkward moment. Suddenly Pope Peter II stood to his feet, striding quickly toward the brazen altar. When Rabbi Cohen saw him coming, he stepped back respectfully. The Pope stood before the altar and said with a voice of authority, "I command fire to fall from the heavens."

The entire crowd looked up toward the sky, wondering, "Could this happen?" Immediately, there was the sound of a rushing wind. Out of the sky came a pillar of fire 25 feet tall. It swept down upon the brazen altar and began to consume the sacrifice. The Temple Mount worshipers were in awe. The Temple Choir began to sing the "Hallelujah Chorus."

All over the Temple Mount, people rejoiced. Some wept unashamedly at the awesome display of power. Others wondered in confusion. "The Pope? Pulling down fire from heaven?"

Chapter Thirty-Eight

Joiner's plan to fight fire with fire—to start a counter religious movement—began to take hold as a result of Pope Peter II calling down fire from heaven. The scene was replayed endlessly on WNN and other major news networks. The effect was electrifying!

The day after the dedication, an article appeared in the *Jerusalem Post* entitled "Is Pope Peter II Elijah?" It was by the same writer that had posed the question a day earlier wondering if Arachev might be the Messiah.

"It makes sense," the writer stated. "The Messiah is supposed to bring peace and security to Israel and facilitate the building of the Temple. All Jews know that. Furthermore, the Prophet Elijah is to precede the revelation of the Messiah. One of the notable miracles that Elijah performed while on earth in biblical times was to pull down fire from heaven. How much clearer could it be? How loudly does God have to speak before we will listen?"

All over Israel, and around the world, people wondered about the amazing events that had transpired. The *Jerusalem Post* articles influenced many people. All the pieces of the puzzle seemed to fit together. How could anyone deny fire falling from heaven?

Yet Jews who knew the Scriptures understood that the Messiah had to be of Jewish descent coming out of the tribe of Judah. Arachev was not Jewish at all. And the Pope being Elijah? It just couldn't be. Yet, fire did fall from heaven.

When Arachev read the article depicting Pope Peter as Elijah, he smiled to himself. "I think the evangelicals have met their match this time," he thought. "Their little revival is just about over. They won't be able to explain this one away!"

After breakfast, he hurried back to his room. He wanted to see what Roger Cornell, the leading prophecy guru, was saying about yesterday's events. He quickly pulled up the website on his laptop. The screen carried the breaking headline:

GREATEST PROPHETIC FULFILLMENT YET!

The False Prophet pulls down fire from heaven just like the prophecies said he would. Revelation 13:13 says regarding the False Prophet: "And he doeth great wonders, so that he maketh fire come down from heaven on the earth in the sight of men, And deceiveth them that dwell on the earth by the means of those miracles which he had power to do in the sight of the beast..."

Ladies and gentlemen, you saw this happen yesterday. You saw the fulfillment of this 2,000-year-old prophecy with your own eyes. Many people in the world are being deceived by this satanically-inspired miracle. However, for those of us who know the prophecies of the Bible, this provides indisputable proof that Pope Paul II is the False Prophet and that Michael Arachev is the Antichrist.

When Michael read what Cornell had written, he was beside himself. "I will stop those evangelicals if it's the last thing I do," he thought to himself. "And I don't care what it takes!" In spite of the fact that the whole world was in awe of him, he couldn't enjoy it as long as these religious radicals continued to speak against his regime.

Michael stayed up late that night. What was he going to do about those religious radicals? They had to be stopped. It was obvious that persuasion would do no good. Nothing could be more persuasive than fire from heaven. Instead, it had the opposite effect.

Arachev instinctively knew that, if left alone, eventually the evangelicals would tear apart his beloved New World Order. The big question was—"What could he do to stop them?"

Around midnight, the answer dawned on him. He had to find a way to force allegiance to his New World Order and the global belief system. He could not have these prophecy fanatics saying that he was the Antichrist and that Pope Peter was the False Prophet. He would have to make allegiance to the New World Order a law.

Fortunately, it would not be difficult to do. After 9/11 and World War III, the people of the world had accepted all kinds of infringements upon their personal freedoms. The wheels for a global ID system had been set in motion after 9/11, but resistance had stalled its implementation until two billion died. After the global holocaust, people were so desperate for security that they willingly accepted the worldwide ID system.

The trick would be taking it to the next level. A worldwide campaign would have to be conducted to convince the world that religious exclusiveness was a poisonous hate crime, which, if not eliminated, would some day trigger World War IV. This theme would become a postulate of the New World Order. Ultimately, anyone who would not pledge allegiance to his leadership would be declared an enemy of the state. That person would either have to be 're-educated' or eliminated.

Chapter Thirty-Nine

Though the Third Temple dedication had been an unmitigated success, there was some residual fallout to be deal with. The Jewish scriptures called for daily sacrifices to be offered each morning and evening. The Jewish rabbis moved immediately to fulfill this requirement.

When the animal rights activists realized that animal sacrifices were being offered daily, demands began to arrive at Arachev's office for him to stop this barbaric practice. Since he was the UN's Secretary General, the Israeli-Palestinian peace agreement made him Mayor of Jerusalem. He was ultimately responsible for what was done on the Temple Mount.

Michael decided to place a phone call to the Pope. He explained the situation and also discussed his idea for solving it. "Your Holiness, as you can see I need your help in order to enact my plan," Arachev stated. "Can you come to Israel right away?"

"For you, Michael, I will be there," the Pope replied immediately,

By the time Pope Peter arrived in Israel, the animal rights demonstrations were in full swing. Picketing around the Temple Mount was ongoing, and things were starting to get ugly. The controversy filled the news, and the demands on the Secretary General's office became increasingly strident. The Secretary General's office put out the announcement that Arachev and Pope Peter would be conducting a joint press conference concerning the Temple Mount crisis.

At ten o'clock the next morning, Arachev and Pope Peter stood on the Temple Mount. Representatives of all the major news services were there as were animal rights activists, many of the rabbis, and a large crowd of interested spectators.

Arachev opened the news conference. "Ladies and gentlemen, all of you are aware of the dispute that has arisen since the dedication of the Temple concerning animal sacrifices. This activity is called for in Jewish scripture, and, in the New World Order, we try to respect all spiritual sensitivities. However, there are other groups, who value all forms of life as sacred, and are terribly offended by these sacrifices.

"When the interests of two equally valid groups come into direct conflict, solutions must be found. I have consulted with the world's most esteemed religious leader, Pope Peter II, concerning our present dilemma. I have asked the Pope to join me today for this news conference. I believe he will have words of wisdom that will solve our present conflict, and will lead to a brighter future for our New World Order. Ladies and gentlemen, please welcome His Holiness, Pope Peter II."

As Pope Peter stepped to the podium, the crowd applauded wildly. Fresh in every person's mind was the unforgettable scene of the pillar of fire falling from the sky, consuming the sacrifice. As the Pope began to speak, the crowd sat in awed silence.

"I consented to come to Israel today because I have a very special announcement to make to you and to the citizens of the world. Throughout human history, we have had an unending series of wars. This has always happened because there was no final authority on earth to rule when conflicting interests resulted in confrontation.

"As you know, most of the religions of the world promise that someday a messiah will come who will provide the answers to all human conflicts. No matter how many laws we create, there is always a problem that is not adequately addressed by our man-made statutes.

"God knew this would be the case. For that reason, He has promised to send the Messiah, or the 5th Buddha, or the Al Mahdi, whatever your particular religion may call him.

"We have entered a new era of human history. War is behind us. National, racial and religious conflicts have been relegated to the dustbin of history. Through the UN's disarmament programs, we are in the process of beating our swords into plowshares and our spears into pruning hooks. Brothers and sisters, we have entered into the messianic era."

With this stunning announcement, a stir went through the crowd. Looks of wonderment were exchanged between those present.

The Pope continued, "As all of you know, there has been much discussion recently concerning whether our global leader Michael Arachev might be the Messiah. I have been sent here today by God to announce to you and the world that Michael Arachev is God's anointed Messiah."

With this stunning announcement, Pope Peter turned toward Arachev. With a wave of his arm, the Pope declared, "Michael Arachev, our Messiah. Receive him!" The crowd leaped to its feet as one, applauding wildly.

As Arachev stepped to the podium, Pope Peter II laid both hands upon his head, "Son of man, Son of God, I now pronounce you Leader of leaders and Ruler of rulers over the earth."

Then Arachev began to speak, "Thank you, Your Holiness. With the help of your spiritual guidance, we will find the path of true peace on earth and goodwill toward all humankind."

Michael continued, "As Pope Peter has said, speculation has been rife that perhaps I am the Messiah. I have avoided this issue until now. The dispute over the animal sacrifices has mandated that I publicly confirm what I have known for a long time. I am your Messiah, your promised, anointed one. This has been my destiny from birth.

"And now for the problem at hand," he said, turning to the Jewish rabbis, "since your Messiah has arrived, you will no longer need to make your sacrifices."

To the animal rights activists, he spoke, "In this conflict, no one has lost and everyone has won. We are all brothers and sisters. If one loses, we all lose. When one wins, we all win. Therefore, embrace your Jewish brothers and sisters and return to your homes in peace."

Suddenly, someone began to say, "Arachev, Messiah. Arachev, Messiah."

Quickly the entire crowd on the Temple Mount was chanting, "Arachev, Messiah. Arachev, Messiah."

Of course, the entire news conference was televised around the world. It was later discovered that, when the chant began, millions around the world joined in.

Chapter Forty

Things were going wonderfully for the New World Order. Everywhere Arachev went, he was greeted with calls of "Arachev, Messiah." The talk show circuit was abuzz with discussion about the dramatic developments. When a caller expressed doubts about Arachev being the Messiah, the caller would always be reminded that Pope Peter II said Arachev was the Messiah, and that "fire from heaven is nothing to argue with."

Arachev couldn't help himself. He had to see what the religious radicals were saying about him. He quickly opened his laptop and located the latest prophecy update. What he saw made his blood boil!

Arachev is the Antichrist!

The Bible prophesies that the Antichrist will stand in the temple of God claiming to be God. This is the sign given that will definitely reveal the identity of the Antichrist. As you know, this has now happened.

The prophecy is found in II Thessalonians 2:3-4: "Let no man deceive you by any means: for that day shall not come, except there come a falling away first, and that man of sin be revealed, the son of perdition; Who opposeth and exalteth himself above all that is called God, or that is worshiped; so that he as God sitteth in the temple of God, shewing himself that he is God."

At his recent press conference, Michael Arachev stood on the Temple Mount, claiming to be the Messiah. Scripture plainly teaches that the Messiah is God. So Arachev, by claiming to be the Messiah, has proclaimed himself God.

Ladies and gentlemen, make no mistake about it. Michael Arachev is the Antichrist.

Arachev was furious! He snapped the lid on his computer shut, his mind racing. If he didn't stop them, they would destroy everything he had spent his life building. He would not let that happen!

Michael placed a call to his good friend, Theodore Joiner. Joiner answered the phone in his usual ebullient style. "Good morning, Michael. How is the Fuehrer of my beloved one-world government today?"

Michael smiled in spite of himself. "You never change, Theodore. I'm calling because I need an unbiased opinion from someone who's not afraid to tell me the truth."

"In sounds to me like you dialed the right number," Joiner replied cockily. "What can I do for you?"

After describing the situation to Joiner, Michael asked, "How do you think I should handle this?"

"Well Michael," Joiner replied, "these people have to be brought under control. The big question is: What is the best way of doing that? The bottom line is money. If you want to get people's attention, hit them in their wallets. After all, when the UN wants to bring a nation under control, it places that nation under economic sanctions. That forces the nation to conform or slowly starve.

"The same thing could be done to individuals. About ninety percent of all financial transactions are already done electronically. It would be simple to change that to one hundred percent. The only people who need cash are those who are doing something illegal anyway. Once people need a number to buy anything or sell anything, bingo, you've got them under your control.

"The next step is a no-brainer. Require a pledge of allegiance to you and the New World Order before they can acquire their global economic ID number. It they refuse, they and their families starve to death. It will surprise you how quickly those religious radicals will see the light!"

Arachev's eyes narrowed. "You know, Theodore," he said thoughtfully. "I think that plan might just work."

Arachev swung into action. The first step was to sell the new program to the people. The best way to do that was through fear.

Stories were published regarding possible terrorist plans against different targets around the world. The discussions always ended up at the same place. The only way to stop global terrorism was to cut off their sources of funding.

People were easily convinced. It was a simple plan: eliminate all cash. Every purchase on earth could now be done electronically. The only ones who needed cash were the terrorists. The world didn't know that Arachev's true target was not the terrorists. It was the evangelicals.

Once all the plans were carefully laid, letters were sent to every individual. The content of the letter was very simple. It read:

Dear World Citizen:
Ever since 9/11, the governments of the world have been waging
an unrelenting war against global terrorism. This plague against

the human race has proven to be more difficult to defeat than we ever thought possible.

In order to ensure the safety of future generations, we are enacting a new level of security to safeguard us all. Beginning on August 9th, all cash will be permanently eliminated. Every financial transaction will be done electronically. This will give us the mechanism to track and eradicate any funding of terrorism.

To receive your economic transaction code, you will need to visit your courthouse prior to August 1st. You will be required to sign a pledge of allegiance to Secretary General Arachev and the New World Order.

Failure to obtain your number by August 1st will result in your inability to participate in the economy. It will also cause your name to be placed on the global list of suspected terrorists.
Yours for peace and safety,

Michael Arachev
UN Secretary General

When the letters arrived around the world, most of the response was positive. Commentators said, "Finally, no more half-measures. This will eliminate the dangerous elements of dissent. We can no longer leave peace to chance. The world is too dangerous."

When the worldwide numbering program was in full swing, Arachev, out of curiosity, went to the prophecy update website.

Warning! Mark of the Beast!
We've been telling you for years that it was coming. Now it is here! By this time, all of you have received your letters ordering you to show up to pledge allegiance to Antichrist Arachev and his satanic one-world government. The Bible clearly describes, in detail, the system now being set up.

You will find this prophecy in Revelation 13:16-17, "And he causeth all, both small and great, rich and poor, free and bond, to receive a mark in their right hand, or in their foreheads: And that no man might buy or sell, save he that had the mark, or the name of the beast, or the number of his name."

Urgent!

This warning is a matter of life and death—eternal life and eternal death. The Bible states that, if you pledge allegiance to the Antichrist and receive his number, you will be eternally lost.

Revelation 14:9-11 says, "...If any man worship the beast and his image, and receive his mark in his forehead, or in his hand, The same shall drink of the wine of the wrath of God, which is poured out without mixture into the cup of his indignation; and he shall be tormented with fire and brimstone in the presence of the holy angels, and in the presence of the Lamb: And the smoke of their torment ascendeth up for ever and ever: and they have no rest day nor night, who worship the beast and his image, and whosoever receiveth the mark of his name."

WHATEVER YOU DO, DO NOT TAKE THE ANTICHRIST'S MARK—EVEN IF IT COSTS YOU YOUR LIFE!

Arachev was angry! He was also puzzled. How could prophecies for everything he was doing appear in the Bible? He quickly rejected the possibility that perhaps there was a God. It was a coincidence, pure and simple!

In the weeks ahead, the vast majority of people complied with the edict of Arachev's New World Order. At the same time, the evangelical revival accelerated at breathtaking speed. "The Letter," as Arachev's letter came to be known, was the best tool the evangelicals had ever gotten their hands on. Christians would show people the prophecy and then show them a copy of the letter. Millions turned to biblical Christianity.

Arachev's patience with the evangelicals had run out. All pretense of allowing religious freedom was suspended. The economic boycott had flushed out the partially committed, but had not fazed the true believers.

Arachev didn't know how they were living. Sympathizers, who themselves had taken the mark, found ways to get their extra food to the Christians. Quickly, a law was passed against this practice. Stories were circulating daily on the Internet of supposed instances of divine provision.

It no longer mattered to Arachev. He was determined to stamp out the evangelicals no matter what it took. He simply would not tolerate their defiance. He issued secret global executive orders to arrest the leaders of the evangelicals on any pretext. Electronic bulletins listing all who had not yet pledged allegiance to the New World Order were sent to every police station around the globe. The orders were clear—obtain the pledge or imprison them.

Because of the vigorous anti-Christian campaign, the jails were soon full. Closed army bases were converted to detention camps where thousands could be incarcerated. But, too many dissenters remained free. It was estimated that evangelical Christians now numbered 700 million.

Then came the dreaded order to all law enforcement agencies: eliminate all religious terrorists who will not recant, immediately. This order should be carried out secretly, since public knowledge of this action might unduly alarm the people.

The full power of governmental structures was mobilized against the Christians. The Internet police eliminated online messages from Christians as soon as they were posted. Little by little, the evangelicals were forced underground. Hundreds of thousands were killed for their refusal to bow to the world government. The defeat of the evangelicals was almost total in the countries of Arachev's power base. However, those who remained continued to function while resisting total absorption into the global government's authority.

Chapter Forty-One

As Arachev stood in front of the mirror, he observed the unmistakable signs of his own mortality: the steely-grey hair, sagging pouches of flesh under his eyes, the deep lines of determination etched into his face. He didn't know how much longer he could function at this level, but he knew he wanted to put the finishing touches on his New World Order.

By this time, most of the world's nations were functioning in harmony with the United Nations. The evangelical problem was not totally solved, but it was coming under control.

There were two major things Arachev still wanted to accomplish. He wanted to rid the world of all nuclear weapons, and he wanted to move the world government headquarters to Jerusalem, making himself King of Jerusalem.

He knew that the nuclear weapons issue could be leveraged into a conflict that would serve as the pretext for the invasion of Israel. To this end, he scheduled a meeting with Israeli Prime Minister Alon.

When Alon arrived, Arachev moved straight to the point. "Prime Minister Alon," he said, "you know how important it is for the world to be free of weapons of mass destruction—nuclear weapons in particular. We have worked very hard to bring peace and safety to Israel. Now it's time for Israel to cooperate with the UN's global disarmament plan."

"Mr. Secretary General," Alon began respectfully, "the people of Israel greatly appreciate your contribution to the peace that we presently enjoy. However, you will not be Secretary General forever. The history of the UN and of the world has been extremely anti-Semitic. If we surrender our ultimate defense, and the nations of the world turn against us as they have in the past, we will face our complete destruction."

Alon continued persuasively, "Mr. Arachev, we have not flaunted our nuclear capability nor acted irresponsibly. However, as a tiny nation living in a hostile sea of forty-two million Arabs, we simply must have a credible means of defense."

Arachev countered, "Mr. Prime Minister, we have entered a new era, the era of globalization. If nations insist on acting unilaterally instead of working in harmony with the world community, we will return to the age of conflict and wars. We cannot allow that to happen."

"I will take this up with my cabinet, Mr. Secretary," Alon replied. "Please be patient with us."

When the two men parted, each understood the other's position perfectly. Alon knew that Arachev sought occasion to move against Israel, and Arachev knew that Alon had no intention of complying with his demands but was merely playing for time.

Arachev immediately focused on building a coalition of states that would participate in the invasion of Israel.

As soon as he arrived back in Israel, Alon called an emergency meeting of his cabinet. When each of the cabinet members had assembled, Alon began, "Ladies and gentlemen, I do not bring a good report from my meeting with the Secretary General. My worst fears have been confirmed. It is obvious to me that Mr. Arachev has already decided to invade Israel using whatever pretext necessary. He is making an issue of our nuclear weapons, but if we were to surrender every one of them, I'm sure he would invent some other reason to move against us." The mood in the cabinet room was somber.

Defense Minister Arens asked the question on everyone's mind, "What is behind this?"

The Prime Minister responded, "It's been the same throughout history. Why have all other leaders of global stature felt compelled to lay claim to Jerusalem? It is a spiritual battle. The god of this world drives them to come here. None of them can resist attempting to place their name where Almighty God has promised to place His own. As soon as I heard Arachev's claim to being the Messiah, I knew this day would come."

The Foreign Minister offered, "Perhaps I can launch a new diplomatic initiative. Maybe the United States will end her isolation to come to our defense."

The Prime Minister shook his head. "We have two choices—surrender, and eventually be herded into concentration camps, or stand and fight."

Defense Minister Arens spoke up, "Mr. Prime Minister, you know we cannot possibly stand up to the armies of the world community."

Alon spoke slowly, "Our choices are simple—surrender and die or fight and depend on our God. I say let's fight. If it comes to it, we will use the Samson Option. If we fail, we will still take down with us all those who come against Jerusalem."

When the cabinet meeting disbursed, every minister knew exactly what needed to be done. Israel prepared for war.

As the other ministers were leaving, Prime Minister Alon spoke to Defense Minister Arens. "Could I have a word with you before you leave?" The Defense Minister stayed behind. Alon spoke quickly, "I know this goes without saying, but put your very best scientists on the job of checking our entire nuclear arsenal. We'll be needing it before this is over." Arens nodded his head soberly as he left the room.

Arachev presented a resolution to the UN Security Council calling for Israel to open her Dimona nuclear installation to international inspection. The resolution passed 14-1 with only the U.S. voting against it. In former days, the resolution would have been killed by the U.S. veto, but now the veto was gone. The measure passed with flying colors.

The world press began to beat the drums for action against Israeli non-compliance with the UN's request. The press argued, "Why should Israel be allowed to have nuclear weapons, when no other nation in the Middle East is allowed to have them? The U.S. invaded Iraq, among other reasons, over the assumption they were assembling weapons of mass destruction. We know that Israel has nuclear weapons. Preferential treatment for Israel must end. It's time to balance the scales."

However, no one bothered to state the obvious. Once Israel no longer had the Samson Option, as her nuclear weapons were called, she was vulnerable to being overrun by the Arabs' whose advantage was in sheer numbers.

Almost no one realized that these issues had become irrelevant. The world's leader, Michael Arachev, had his sights set on making Jerusalem his own.

Once the anti-Israeli campaign began, it rapidly gained momentum. All of the latent anti-Semitism around the world came boiling to the surface. Arachev smiled to himself. "This won't be difficult at all," he thought with deep satisfaction.

An international coalition was formed. Many nations had been waiting for this day. The abiding hatred against the Jews was strong and bitter. The coalition included Libya, Iran, Ethiopia, Turkey and Russia, among others.

As tensions built between Israel and the UN, the religious awakening, that was already progressing in Israel, accelerated dramatically. The Jewish people realized they were going to need God's help as never before.

Once Arachev's mind was made up to invade Israel, he moved without hesitation. If anything threatened to get in his way, a burning anger bordering on hatred would well up within him. It was his destiny to rule the world, and the time had come for him to assert total global control.

He found himself seized with a burning passion to establish his global headquarters in Jerusalem. Michael could already envision his new headquarters. It would be a building without rival—the tallest in Jerusalem. On the outside and high enough to be seen all over the city would be the words, "Michael Arachev—Emperor of the New World Order." Michael thought to himself, "God said that He would put His name in Jerusalem, but I haven't seen it yet. Once my name is there, the whole world will see it. I'll make sure of that."

The day of the invasion couldn't arrive quickly enough for Arachev. He had no doubt concerning the outcome.

The first thrust of the attack swept down from the north. The heavy Russian armor blasted its way through the initial Israeli defenses. The battle was fully joined when the forces of the world community arrived at the Plain of Megiddo. The intensity of the warfare exceeded any military conflict in all of world history. Tanks were rolling, and jets were screaming overhead. Men were dying, and blood was flowing like water! It was everything that Armageddon had promised to be!

The preponderance of military strength enjoyed by the enemy began to push Israel backward into the Jordan valley towards Jerusalem. The fierce and inhuman level of conflict drove men to the brink of insanity. They were fighting for their lives, and hundreds of thousands were dying.

Arachev had estimated that the campaign against Israel would last about eight days. As it turned out, he was right. Michael had instructed the commanding general of the coalition forces to notify him when ultimate victory was at hand. Arachev wanted to be present when Jerusalem became his own.

The call came at 11:03 a.m. "Mr. Secretary General," the commander said, "I expect the total capitulation of Jerusalem at about twelve noon."

The chauffer of the Hummer in which Arachev was riding surged ahead toward the frontlines. Michael wanted to arrive at Jerusalem in time to personally accept the surrender of Israel's commanding general.

When they came around the side of the Mount of Olives, the military radio reported that the Israeli Defense Forces had just run out of ammunition. "We're going in to capture the Temple Mount," the commander of the Global Forces announced.

Arachev's chauffer swung the Hummer toward the lookout on the Mount of Olives. It would be the perfect vantage point for the UN Secretary General to witness the capture of Jerusalem. Since the Israelis were out of ammunition, Michael thought it would be safe to step outside the vehicle to witness the unfolding drama. He watched in exaltation as the Global Forces climbed up the portable ladders that had been quickly affixed to the Temple Mount walls.

As Arachev watched, he thought to himself, "This is the ultimate! This is the moment I have waited for all of my life. This is my destiny—the reason I was born."

At that moment, an effervescent brightness began to surround him. All of the dark self-confidence that he had enjoyed since yielding himself to Satan, suddenly melted away. Turning to see the source of the ever-increasing brightness, he found himself face to face with a brilliant white-clad figure on a powerful white horse. His face shone with a brilliance that Michael could not bear to look upon. Across his chest was a name emblazoned, "THE WORD OF GOD."

Suddenly, a voice like thunder emanated from the rider of the white horse, "Michael Arachev, thou shalt worship the Lord thy God, and Him only shalt thou serve." The power of those words engulfed him like a paralyzing whirlwind. Every bit of strength in his body drained from him. He found himself kneeling before the one on the white horse.

The last thing he heard himself say was, "Jesus Christ, You are the King of Kings. You are Lord!"

"...At the name of Jesus every knee should bow...and *that* **every tongue should confess that Jesus Christ** *is* **Lord..."**

Philippians 2:10-11

Endtime Magazine

World events from a biblical perspective
America's leading prophecy magazine

Irvin Baxter

Publisher Editor

Presenting tomorrow's news today!
Subscribe today!

www.endtime.com

Understanding
the Endtime

Level One
Bible prophecy series authored by

Irvin Baxter

Ten Lessons

1. United States & Other Modern Nations in the Bible
2. New World Order Is World Government
3. Mideast Peace–Prelude to Armageddon
4. The Four Horsemen
5. The Roman Empire Revived
6. Antichrist & False Prophet
7. Mark of the Beast
8. The Coming One-World Religion
9. How to Enter the Kingdom of God
10. The Rapture

Three Ways to Learn
Video Series • Cassette Series • Study Manual

Four Ways to Teach
Flip Chart • Transparecies • Slides • Video Series

You will understand prophecy like never before!

Also by
Irwin Baxter

THE CHINA WAR
AND
THE THIRD TEMPLE

What will the world be like the day after one-third of the earth's population is snuffed out in a horrible holocaust?

An unprecedented cry for a system of global government that can enforce peace and security will be heard around the world. This time of global emergency will be the perfect backdrop for the rise of a world leader with answers. The personage that will respond to this call for global leadership will be the man that has stood silently in the wings of the world stage for years - the Antichrist.

ISBN 0-7684-3043-7